What Reviewers Are Saying:

Stand-In Mom

Romantic Times Book Reviews (4 1/2 Stars)
"charming romance"

and

"a runaway good read"
"rich in emotional detail"

The Marriage Solution
"a sweet story of love and parenting"

Santa Dear
"an uplifting story that will give you the holiday spirit
any time of the year"

Other books by Megan Kelly:

HOLLY & IVEY, Christmas in Stilton, Book Two

Love in Little Tree series
THE WEDDING RESCUE
RUNAWAY BRIDE
BABY MAKES THREE
COMING HOME
GHOST OF A CHANCE (novella)

Returning Home Romance series:
FIXER-UPPER

Harlequin American Romances:
  MARRYING THE BOSS AR 1206
  THE FAKE FIANCEE AR 1219
  THE MARRIAGE SOLUTION   AR 1356
  STAND-IN MOM   AR 1371

Please visit Megan's website at megankellybooks.com.

For a free short story and to keep up to date on news and releases, sign up for her newsletter on the website.

Santa Dear

Christmas in Stilton
Book One

Megan Kelly

Enjoy the Season
Megan Kelly

As always, for my husband, with love.

All rights reserved.
Print Copyright 2014 by Megan Kelly
eBook Copyright 2011 by Megan Kelly

Cover design by The Killion Group, Inc.

ISBN 978-0-9886017-1-0

No part of this book may be reproduced or transmitted in any form by any means, electronic or mechanical, including photocopying, recording, or by any information storage and retrieval systems, without permission of the author.

This is a work of fiction. Any references to historical events, real people, or real locales are used fictitiously. Other names, characters, places and incidents are the product of the author's imagination, and any resemblance to actual events, locales or persons, living or dead, is entirely coincidental.

CHAPTER ONE

"I need a man," Trish Howell said. "Can I borrow your husband?"

Jenny McIntire gawked for a moment then snapped her mouth shut. "What for?"

"For about an hour, maybe less. I wouldn't ask, but I'm pretty desperate." Trish lowered her gaze to Jenny's kitchen table, trying to keep a straight face. "I know Bart has experience. I just hope he's good enough to fake it."

"I doubt he'll have to fake it." Jenny smirked. "And I'd be surprised if it took him an hour."

Trish laughed. "I need him to play Santa for Tyler."

Jenny smiled in response. "Oh. That's okay then. Did Tyler find out about Santa from his friends?"

Trish nodded and took Tyler's letter from her purse. She passed it across the table. The words were branded on her heart.

Dear Santa,
My frends say you arent real, your just a story. Like my dad.
If your you, please wak me up wen you come to my howse. I want to meet you.
Your frend, Tyler.
Ps. Dont forget I want a reel bike.

Jenny laughed, and Trish leaned forward with a scowl. "What's so funny?"

"Isn't it amazing that kids never add their last names when they write Santa? As though Santa will automatically know which Tyler this is." Jenny's grin melted under the heat of Trish's gaze. "Sorry. I didn't know you were taking this so seriously."

Trish couldn't believe Jenny had missed the point. "Of course I am."

"All kids doubt Santa sooner or later. You'll get through it."

"This is different, Jenny. I can deal with scraped knees or an upset stomach. But this ..." Trish looked away.

"Ahh." Jenny nodded, her curls bouncing on her shoulders. "Being a single mom is the pits when there's a crisis."

The familiar ache of loneliness swept through Trish. "Having to make every decision by yourself is always the pits."

"And you always handle it perfectly, honey. Just like you

will this time. You're the great organizer, the great fixer. I have faith in you."

"Well, I don't want to be 'the great fixer' anymore," Trish said. "I wish I had someone to rely on for a change. It's awful to say, but at times like this, I could almost hate Duke for dying."

"From what you've told me about Duke, I have to wonder how much help he would have been."

"Probably not much." Trish straightened and tucked a strand of unruly red hair behind her ear. "But since he isn't here, I guess I'd better think of something. It's already the week before Thanksgiving. What would you do?"

"Praise Tyler for his spelling? You have to admit, he spells really well for just being in kindergarten."

"Look closer at the writing, Jen. I think Nick helped him."

"My Nick?" Jenny snatched up the extra-wide-ruled paper and scanned it. "This is atrocious for a second-grader. I can see we'll be sitting down with extra spelling work over Thanksgiving break."

"How old was Nick when he–" Trish dropped her tone to a whisper even though they were alone in the house. "Learned about Santa?"

"Ten or eleven, I hope," Jenny whispered in return.

Trish groaned. "He doesn't know yet? I don't want to

perpetuate a lie if it's time for Tyler to learn the truth. On the other hand, he *is* only five. That's awfully young for a kid to lose Santa, too."

"Too?" Jenny paused a moment, searching Trish's expression. "Is it Tyler doubting Santa that's bothering you or the line about his dad just being a story he's heard?"

Trish wrapped her hands around her tea cup and glanced over at Tyler's letter on the table. "That really got to me, Jen."

Jenny squeezed Trish's arm. "Are Duke's parents still giving you a hard time about Tyler?"

"Jock hasn't said anything."

"What did Miriam say?"

Trish grimaced. "I don't want to get into this right now."

"She's so critical about the way you're raising Ty. Every time she mentions her friend, Lucille, getting custody of her granddaughter–" Jenny smacked the table. "I just want to shake her. Can't she see what a wonderful job you're doing?"

Warm gratitude flooded through Trish. "Thank you. Miriam only sees what suits her purposes."

"Why do you put up with her?"

"She's Duke's mother. Even though Duke's been gone for four years, I still think of her and Jock as my in-laws. But whatever our relationship is, they'll always be Ty's grandparents."

"If you don't tell me what she said, I'm going to imagine the worst."

"Same old thing."

Jenny snorted. "Yeah, I can imagine. You forget. I know the woman." Her face scrunched. "We never get to see Tyler."

Trish smiled as Jenny mimicked Miriam's long-suffering tone.

"You never call," Jen continued. "We feel like we're losing touch with our grandson."

Trish smiled wider but didn't interrupt.

"You work too hard at your store. Poor Tyler is being neglected."

Trish laughed outright. "Were you listening in on our phone conversation?"

"No, I've just seen her martyr act before. Remember Ty's birthday party?"

Trish shuddered. Miriam had cried throughout the entire celebration because Duke would never see Tyler grow up. "If you hadn't kept her in my bedroom, she would have ruined the party for Ty." She sighed. "I've invited her and Jock over for Thanksgiving dinner. I hope that'll help."

"She'll just complain about being usurped as the cook."

"Miriam tends to get more emotional around the holidays. I can understand that. Duke was their only child, and Tyler is their last link to him."

"And they're going to tighten the chain that links them until you choke."

"Now, Jenny." Trish patted her hand. "I appreciate your loyalty, but I don't think it'll be a problem. I've always handled them in the past. This year won't be any different." She grinned. "I'm the great fixer, remember?"

Jenny leaned back in her chair. Her platinum hair swung into place around her thin, heart-shaped face. The color would have been too harsh on another woman, but Jenny's natural warmth radiated from her dark brown eyes. "If you need me to run interference or something, just call."

"Thanks, but I just have to figure out what to tell, or not tell, Tyler."

"Okay, here's what I think. The question isn't whether Tyler's old enough to learn about Santa. The question is what would make both of you happy?"

"I guess I'll need your husband, after all."

"You're welcome to borrow him." Jenny grinned. "But just to play Santa. You're right to worry about him faking it. Ty might recognize Bart under the beard and hat."

"I'm afraid so too." Trish growled with frustration. "This is a no-win situation. I can't bring his father back from the dead anymore than I can get Santa to visit."

She stopped abruptly and sat silent for a moment, staring

past Jenny as half-formed ideas swirled in her head. "Well, now, wait a minute. Maybe I can."

Jenny shivered and looked back over her shoulder where Trish's gaze was fixed. "I sure hope you're talking about Santa Claus coming."

"What?" Trish blinked. "I'll hire a Santa to visit Ty."

"Hire who?"

Trish popped up like a champagne cork. She paced quickly around the long kitchen, too excited to sit still. Suddenly the smell of the beef roasting in the oven made her hungry rather than queasy. "This is great. I can get one of those department store guys. I'll probably have to pay him extra to come over late on Christmas Eve, but it'll be worth it."

"Whoa, girl. Sit down."

Trish spun toward Jenny. "Why? What's the matter?"

"You're not thinking clearly. You can't invite a strange man into your house in the middle of the night."

"Oh." Trish dropped onto the chair, deflated by reality.

"Especially not on Christmas Eve, when you'll have all those presents he could steal, not to mention what he might do to you first."

Trish slouched in her seat.

Jenny gave her a smug smile. "But I have the perfect solution."

Trish cocked her head with wary skepticism. "I'm well-acquainted with the nature of your solutions. They tend to involve me meeting some man."

"Just hear me out."

Trish sighed in resignation. "Who is he?"

Jenny had the grace to blush, but she charged on nevertheless. "Sam Carrow. He's Bart's best friend from high school." She shot Trish an annoyed glare. "The one I've been trying to fix you up with for three months now."

Trish spooned some sugar into her cup, wondering how she could change the subject. She missed the intimacy of marriage, but, as for trusting a man again ... "I'm not ready yet."

"Duke's been dead more than four years."

"I'm too busy." She didn't intend to let Jenny make her feel guilty.

"Sure you are." Jenny rolled her eyes. "Okay, we need to plan the fine details of Santa's visit."

"Why would Bart's friend agree to interrupt his Christmas Eve to play Santa for my son?"

"Because he's a nice guy. Don't you remember me telling you about him?"

Trish evaded her probing stare. She never listened when Jenny played matchmaker. Instead, she frantically searched her mind for an excuse her friend would buy. The only male she could handle right now was a five-year-old bundle of mischief. She'd rather not hear Jen extol the virtues of some "perfect" man. She snatched a bit of Jen's remark from mid-air. "Of course I listen. He's that friend Bart's known so long."

"Right."

Trish released a sigh. Close call.

"He's staying with us for the holidays. And he's not working right now, so I know he'll be free to do it. He's so good with kids, he's sure to make a great Santa."

Trish set her jaw. "Don't start pushing him at me as a daddy candidate."

"What did I say?"

"'He's so good with kids,'" she echoed.

Jenny waved away Trish's annoyance. "If I don't find somebody for you, you'll never be as happy as I am with Bart. You'll never have anyone to rely on at crisis time."

Hearing her own words repeated back to her made Trish wince. "Let's just stick to this guy playing Santa."

"Did I mention he's filling in at the preschool this year instead of Bart?"

"No, you didn't. Are you afraid Heather will recognize her daddy?"

Jenny tossed her head in a haughty manner, a perfect mimicry of her daughter. "Well, she *is* three and a half now."

Trish laughed. "I remember Tyler at that age. So

independent." She considered the situation. Sam could borrow the costume from the preschool Jenny owned. Ty didn't know him. If Sam agreed, it just might work. "Poor Bart. How's he taking being replaced as Santa?"

Jenny laughed. "You'd think he was one of the kids at my preschool, opening his lunch to discover there's no dessert."

Trish shook her head. "I've never seen anyone enjoy playing a role as much as Bart does being Santa. It's hard to believe he's a lawyer."

"He says it's the one time of the year people actually like him. No one tells vicious Santa jokes."

Trish sipped her tea. Although she had no intention of getting involved with Sam, it was hard not to be curious. "So, Sam is staying with you for the holidays. Where does he live?"

Jenny's eyes brightened, making Trish regret showing any interest. "Here in Cloverdale. He's been working around the Stilton area for a long time, going wherever residential development is booming."

Trish nodded at the mention of the sister city. Cloverdale, where she and Jen lived, and Stilton, where Trish had her store, were really one community separated by politics. With the economy in such straits, development wasn't "booming" anywhere. That would be rough on a construction worker or carpenter or whatever Sam's specialty was. Too many people were laid off now.

"Bart and I were thrilled when he decided to settle nearby this summer. I'd never have suggested you meet him if a relationship meant you'd move away."

Trish leveled a look at Jenny. "This Santa thing isn't more matchmaking, is it?"

Jenny's face expressed total innocence. "Who, me?"

"Jenny–"

"Of course it's not. You need a Santa. I have a Santa. What could be simpler?"

Trish rolled her eyes.

"Believe what you will." Jenny crossed her arms piously, her white turtleneck adding to her saintly image.

"Doesn't Sam have family to visit over the holidays?"

"They're not close."

Trish frowned, unsure of her meaning. Was the relationship strained or did his family live far away? "If he lives here, why is he staying with you?"

"Oh, Trish." Jenny reached across the table and clasped her hand. "You should see his place. There are holes in the walls, and some of the flooring is torn up. I doubt if it's safe to walk around over there. There was no way I could enjoy Christmas with Sam living like that. What if he has to turn off his heat for some reason? It may not come back on."

"No heat?" Trish blinked. That was no small matter in central Illinois. Recent newspaper articles reminded readers of last year's tragedies throughout the Midwest and asked for donations of coats and heaters. People froze to death each winter, despite the emergency shelters.

Sam wasn't working. His house sounded positively dangerous, with parts of the floors missing. The poor guy. No job and practically homeless. Trish's heart went out to him. "How long have you known him?"

"I met Sam and Bart at a party Bart's fraternity brothers threw for his birthday. They invited all the sororities." Jenny chuckled and shook her head. "Sam didn't go to school there and sort of crashed the event. Bart's lucky we met before I saw Sam."

Trish grinned. "Oh, now I get it. Since you fell in love with Bart, you want to foist this other guy off on me. I get the loser?"

Again.

The word hung over the table. Trish swallowed hard against the lump that formed in her throat. Was it guilt? Self-pity? Regret? Duke hadn't been a loser, she reasoned. He'd just lacked ambition, straining their finances, and then straining her patience with his lies. If she ever got involved again–and that was a very big if–it wouldn't be with another user.

Casting blindly for something–anything–to say, Trish heard the words come from her mouth. "I'll take him." Jenny's wide eyes made her add, "For Santa. I'll hire him."

"Hire him?" Jenny frowned, her brow furrowing. "I doubt if he'd take money for this. He'll be insulted if you even offer."

"But he's... he's..." Trish gestured vaguely with her hand. She couldn't say "needy." Even needy people had their pride, usually more than their share.

"He's what?"

"He's giving up Christmas Eve."

"Sam won't care. He won't take payment for helping out a friend."

"But I'm a stranger."

"After ten minutes with Sam you won't be."

Trish heard the door to the enclosed back deck being opened, followed by a deep male voice and footsteps.

"The guys are back from the Ivey Christmas tree farm with the kids," Jenny said. "We'll ask Sam right away."

*

Sam Carrow opened the door to the McIntires' kitchen. Little three-year-old Heather rode on his back, her chubby toddler arms clasped around his neck.

Which probably explained why he couldn't breathe when he caught sight of the woman at Jenny's table. She looked like an angel who'd come early for the holidays.

Sam stared at her. Sparkling green eyes dominated her oval face. A nose that could only be described as "pert" topped shiny pink lips. Pale freckles dusted her creamy cheeks. Strands of pure gold shone through her dark red hair. He stood mesmerized.

Judging by her wide-eyed stare and parted lips, she didn't appear unaffected seeing him.

"Trish!" Heather's shriek pierced Sam's ear. "Let me down, Uncle Sam. Let me down." The little girl kicked and struggled for freedom while he eased her to the floor. As soon as her toes touched, Heather catapulted across the room.

So, this is Jenny's friend. From what Sam remembered hearing about her drive to succeed with her business, she didn't qualify as an angel. Not in his book. He shrugged off his momentary disappointment.

"Whoa, muffin," Trish said with a laugh.

He watched as she caught Heather in her arms for a tight hug. Trish wrinkled her nose and leaned back with wide eyes. Sam grinned, remembering how the little girl had spent her day. When Heather burrowed her face into Trish's chest, Trish rested her cheek on the girl's hair.

His breath snagged in his chest with bittersweet pressure. They looked absolutely beautiful together, like Madonna and

Child. Trish obviously loved the girl with the same fierceness Heather showered upon her.

"I dint know you was coming," Heather cried in apparent delight.

Trish drew away and looked at the child with a gentle, teasing smile. "Would you have stayed home if you'd known?"

Heather's hair bounced in a vigorous affirmative. Then her nearly black curls slowly shifted from left to right and back again. "No. Well, most times. But today, I goed out with Uncle Sam. We picked out a tree to be cutted down for our very own."

"My gracious." Trish lifted her face, her solemn expression belied by the humor shining in her bright eyes. "Hello."

Sam stiffened, drawn against his will. "Hi."

Trish cleared her throat. "Did you get to help choose the tree?"

"Oh, no. Heather and Nick found their tree. But they're going to let me help chop it down in three weeks."

"How nice of them." Jenny winked at her daughter. "Uncle Sam does the work, and you kids have the fun."

"Hey, I had a great time at the Ivey tree farm," Sam said. "We never had a real tree when I was little, let alone one we got to choose and chop down ourselves."

Heather's eyes grew wide. "You never had a Christmas

tree?"

Touched by her concern, Sam smiled gently. "We had a silver one, Heather. It had a light at the bottom with a cover that spun around to make the tree different colors."

"I like just green trees best," the girl said solemnly.

"So do I." He'd hated that tree. Every year he'd worried, sure that Santa would never leave presents under a tree so ugly. His mother loved the tree–no mess, no fuss, no expense.

"Where are Bart and Nick?" Jenny asked.

"They goed to get some milk." Heather flung herself into her mother's arms.

"Phew! What have you gotten into, young lady?"

"I rolled in some hay and stepped in some goat poo."

Trish laughed. "Is that what I smell?"

Jenny leveled a look at Sam. "Goat poo?"

"We cleaned it off," he put in quickly. "The Christmas tree farm also had animals to pet. I can't smell anything but dinner. Is that roast? I'm starving."

"I fed some goats milk in a baby bottle," Heather went on, spoiling his diversion. "It spitted up all over me. Then another goat jumped up on me, and I falled on the ground." Heather laughed, hardly able to catch her breath. "Three goats climbed on top of me, trying to get the bottle before Uncle Sam and Daddy pulled me out."

When Jenny glared at him, Sam choked back his laughter. He shrugged and smiled, hoping it was charming enough to get him off the hook.

Jenny eyed Heather. "No wonder you smell like wild animals."

"No wonder Bart went to the store." Trish's wry comment sparked a chain of laughter.

Her gaiety drew Sam's gaze. She averted her eyes, leaving Sam confused.

"To the tub with you, young lady." Jenny stood and held Heather in front of her at arm's length as the child giggled and squirmed, trying to "get goat smell all over Mommy." At the doorway, Jen turned back. "Trish Howell, meet Sam Carrow. Sam, Trish. I'll scoot this little one upstairs. You two talk before Nick gets home."

Jenny disappeared, leaving Sam to stare after her. "Why do we have to talk before Nick gets here?" He shrugged off his jacket and stepped out to hang it on the deck. Without the sheepskin jacket, the chill air swept over him. He shut the door quickly so Trish wouldn't get cold.

Taking Jenny's vacant chair across from Trish, he smiled politely, wondering why she seemed uncomfortable now they were alone. She glanced away when he caught her looking at him. "I hope I don't smell like goats, too."

"Were you wrestling them as well?"

"No." Sam's laughter echoed in the room. He pulled in his legs, conscious of his height and bulk compared to Trish's delicate, feminine frame. He hadn't felt this overgrown and awkward since his teen years. He brushed a piece of crumbled leaf from the arm of his white sweater. "I'll have to ask Jenny if she can get these grass stains out."

Trish wrapped her hands around her cup.

"I've heard so much about you from Bart and Jenny," he said, "I feel I already know you."

She cleared her throat. "Yes, I'm afraid that's probably true. Jenny does like to talk."

He shrugged. "She likes you. And, while I'm thinking about it, congratulations on your store. Jenny says it's doing very well."

"Thanks." Trish beamed. "I've worked very hard there."

The familiar dread settled heavy in his chest. *Not another one.* Career-driven women gravitated to him like termites to a wood pile. "You have a son, too, if I remember right. What do you do with him while you're working?"

"He's in kindergarten now, so I have more freedom."

Sam winced inwardly. Did Trish consider her son a burden, keeping her from doing the things she wanted to do? Sam thought of his mother. *Déjà vu* all over again.

"My assistant, Candy, used to babysit Tyler in the back

of the store, in what's now our lunch room. We still keep an area for him to work on his school papers."

A sour taste invaded Sam's mouth. He could imagine Trish parceling out her time, playing with her child until the bell over the door rang, announcing more customers.

"I should get going." She stood and pushed her chair under the table.

"It was nice meeting you," he lied. Meeting her had stirred unwanted memories of his neglectful mother and the pain of his childhood. No matter how pretty Trish was, he wouldn't go down that path again.

*

Fifteen minutes later, Trish slammed the door to her house, glad Tyler was staying overnight at Candy's. *Well, great.* Jenny would ask Sam to play Santa for Tyler. Her son's doubts would be erased, at least until next year.

That was what she'd wanted, right?

A too-handsome, too-likeable, too-sexy man coming over late on Christmas Eve, after Tyler was in bed.

She flung her purse at the couch, picturing Sam Carrow's thick, dark blond hair and those marvelous navy-blue eyes. She pressed her fist against her lips, recalling how she'd wanted Sam to kiss her, how she'd repeatedly pulled her gaze from his beautiful mouth. The man was more tempting than a pan of fudge and just as bad for her.

Dammit.

Sam seemed perfectly happy to be living with Jenny and Bart, letting someone else take care of him. All her compassion for an unemployed man living in a house ready to be condemned had evaporated as Sam joked about Jenny feeding him and washing his clothes. He was a user, a taker. She couldn't be attracted to a man like that. Not again.

She wouldn't be.

*

"Where did Trish go?"

Sam glanced up from unpacking a duffle bag in the guest room. He'd brought a few more things from his house so sawdust and plaster wouldn't settle into the creases of everything he'd need for the next few weeks. "Home."

Jenny crossed the room and leaned against the wall by the dresser. "What did you think of her?"

He shrugged. Jenny's nonchalant pose didn't fool him. The woman was in attack mode.

"I'd hoped you'd like each other."

Sam grimaced. "So I gathered."

"Don't give me that look. I'm entitled to set up my friends. I want you to have the happiness Bart and I have found."

"And you thought Trish was the right woman for me?"

He shook his head.

"Okay, putting that aside, there's something else. She needs someone to play Santa for her son. Tyler has doubts, and we think he's too young to lose faith in Santa. I suggested you."

Sam met her gaze levelly. "I'm not interested in her or in being Santa Claus for her. Don't try fixing us up, Jen."

Jenny didn't appear a bit ashamed for matchmaking. "Trish is really nice. We've been friends for three years, when she enrolled Tyler in my preschool."

Sam turned away but said nothing. He wouldn't fault a woman for putting her son in preschool, learning to play with others and getting ready for school. Yet he wondered if Trish had jumped at the chance to get Tyler someplace so she could concentrate on her business. *Freedom*, she'd called it.

"She's been alone too long," Jenny continued as he grabbed another shirt from the bag, "raising her son on her own. She's struggled to make her store a success and put bread on the table."

"So she needs a rich husband?"

"It would solve a lot of her problems if she were to marry a wealthy man next time."

Sam drew in a quiet breath, hurt. "I thought better of you, Jenny."

"She doesn't need just the rich part, Sam. She needs

someone to take care of her for a change. She's a really nice woman, if you'd just give her a chance."

"I'm not in the market for a gold-digger."

Laying a hand on his forearm, Jenny met his gaze and held it. "Not all women are like Sherry."

An image of his ex-girlfriend came unbidden to his mind. Sleek. Beautiful. Cold. Living together suited Sherry. She liked being seen at the places he'd taken her. Until he'd proposed.

She'd refused, said planning a wedding would sidetrack her from getting ahead in the corporation. She'd have been satisfied with continuing their relationship as it stood, but she needed to concentrate on her career. Sam had declined and moved to Cloverdale, staying near his business in Stilton.

He wouldn't get mixed up with another woman who put her career before her family, even Jenny's best friend. His mother and Sherry had been lessons enough. He would find the ideal woman someday, but it wasn't Trish Howell.

"Tell her to look elsewhere for Santa *and* for a husband."

CHAPTER TWO

"Tyler Zachary Howell," Trish muttered through her teeth when she located his favorite plastic horse. "I'm going to wring your cute little neck!"

She tossed the toy in the sink and dried her cold hands on a towel. Glancing around the flooded bathroom, Trish shook her head. Strangling him wouldn't teach her son not to flush his toys down the toilet, although she didn't believe he'd done this intentionally.

She was more concerned that Tyler hadn't told her what happened. She raised him to value honesty above all else. His beloved Horsey would be dried and set on a shelf in plain sight, where Ty would see it and remember why he wasn't allowed to play with it. Hopefully, after a week, he'd have learned his lesson.

In the meantime, Trish had two inches of water to clean and a toilet to reassemble. A practical woman, she reached for the phone. "Jenny, hi. It's me again."

"Did you locate the problem?"

Trish glowered. "I sure did."

"Oh-oh. I don't like your tone. Should Tyler stay here for dinner?"

"And maybe even for breakfast tomorrow. It was Horsey."

Jenny's chuckle echoed through the line. "I could have guessed that. Ty got all teary-eyed earlier when Nick asked him why he didn't bring Horsey. After you called about the bathroom flooding, I had a nasty suspicion that Horsey had found a new watering trough."

"I'm so glad you're amused. Can I borrow your wet/dry vac?"

"Of course."

"I hate to ask, but could Bart bring it over if he's not busy? I still have the toilet to fix."

"Bart's not–"

Trish listened to the silence for a moment, more than familiar with the difficulties of having a phone conversation with a child in the house. "Jen?"

"Don't worry about putting the toilet back together. Help is on the way."

"You're a pal. And thank Bart, too."

"Mmm-mm."

Knowing Jenny as she did, Trish should have expected the help that came. But when the knock sounded on the door she'd left unlocked, she hollered, "Down here, Bart."

When a male outline entered her peripheral vision, she didn't think about her hair bunched into a ponytail, her worn denim cut-offs, her damp, navy T-shirt or her lack of a bra.

Until she saw Sam.

She really should have known. She'd have to wring Jenny's neck, too. Trish sighed, noticing how great he looked in a worn denim jacket and even older jeans. "Hi. Jenny didn't tell me you were coming."

Sam's eyebrows rose. On him, even that looked sexy. During the last seven days apart, Trish had convinced herself Sam couldn't be as attractive as she remembered. At least, she *thought* she'd convinced herself.

"Jenny asked me to bring over the shop vac. Kind of looks like you need it."

"I asked for Bart... Never mind." Trish grinned. "I guess this time, I'm the one who needs to apologize for the way I look–and probably smell."

Her giggle died even as Sam laughed. She closed her eyes in utter mortification, stifling a groan. What was she saying? Making jokes about the way he dressed and smelled. She just had trouble thinking of Sam as one of the needy. Meeting his warm blue eyes, she said, "I'm sorry. That was clumsy."

"That's okay. It's not as though I always smell like goats. Seldom do I have to rescue three-year-old, fair maidens from such dire peril."

"You're very nice." Why, then, had he refused to play Santa for Tyler? Jenny hadn't given her a reason. Trish assumed Sam hadn't told Jen why. He'd just said no.

"Thanks." Sam's gaze locked with hers for a moment, then he shifted his weight. "I have the shop vac in my truck."

Trish glanced back at the toilet she'd managed to reassemble. Blowing a wisp of hair out of her eyes with an irritated sigh, she wished she'd waited for help. She could have spent more time with Sam while they fixed the toilet.

Very romantic, Trish.

Her breath caught in her throat. She had no time to think of romance now. And with Sam, of all men? She already knew enough about him to avoid further involvement. He was too much like Duke.

"I'll bring it in and vacuum up the water for you," Sam offered. "You could go get out of those wet things." His eyes ran over her.

And lingered.

Trish barely heard him swallow over the pounding of her heart. The images of them together flashed through her mind and left her speechless. Her face flamed. She hadn't thought this way in years. She hadn't felt this way in years, either.

"I mean, you could get dry," Sam said. "Changed. Put on something more..." He waved his hand vaguely. "Something else."

The heat in the room should have evaporated all the water. Trish quickly turned away and crossed her arms over her chest to hide her body's reaction.

She offered Sam a bright smile, which she hoped looked more natural than it felt. "Thanks for bringing it over, but I'll clean up. There's hot tea upstairs or you can make some instant coffee, if you'd like. I've already turned on the water." She bit her lip to stop babbling. "I'll be up in a few minutes."

After I change. She watched him walk through the laundry area, hoping she had some clean clothes down here. She definitely needed more clothes on. More armor.

More common sense.

*

Sam took her the vac, then climbed the steps, glad to escape the moist heat of Trish's bathroom. He regretted that she wouldn't let him sweep up the water, but not as much as he regretted his wayward thoughts.

"You're losing your touch." Sam found a mug and filled it with milk. He sat at the small round table in the kitchen and propped his head on his hand.

What had happened down there? In the midst of toilet overflow, no less. His words had conjured up an image of Trish, desire making her eyes glow darkly green. Had Trish noticed his response? Naturally, she drew his attention. She was gorgeous. But Sam couldn't recall the last time the mere thought of a woman naked had affected him like this. Probably, he reasoned, the attraction only seemed stronger because he didn't want to be drawn to Trish. Forbidden fruit and all that.

Hearing the vacuum motor turn off, Sam opened the cookie tin and tried to clear his thoughts. He remained seated, guessing by the adamant way she'd rebuffed his earlier offers that Trish would prefer to empty the vac herself. It wasn't a strenuous task, but Sam fidgeted in his seat, finding it harder than he expected to just sit by without helping.

To distract himself, Sam studied Trish's house, trying to find out more about her. The appliances were an ugly avocado green, at least thirty years old. The linoleum was cracked. The kitchen served double-duty as the eating area.

Sam glanced through the opening into the living room. Quilts graced the worn furnishings. Across the back of the sofa lay a white quilt with brown and yellow stars. Four matching pillows rested in the adjacent wing chair and love seat, two with yellow stars and two with brown stars. A smaller, pale yellow quilt covered the love seat.

His gaze caught on a large quilted wall-hanging behind the sofa, depicting a field of horses and a rippling, tree-lined brook. If Trish made her living creating art like this, she must pour a lot of her energy and passion into each project. She'd have little time left over.

Just like his mother. Just like Sherry. The comparisons reminded him why his physical attraction to Trish could go no further.

The stairs creaked, announcing Trish's arrival. Armed with the reminders of his past, Sam figured he was immune to her. She stepped into the kitchen in different clothes. A thin black sweater deepened her green eyes and made her face look even creamier and softer to the touch. Worn jeans hugged her legs. Sam swallowed dryly. Shiny pink toenails peeked out from under dark blue denim.

All the blood in his upper body rushed south, leaving his head spinning. *Over painted toenails?* He was losing it.

"I'm glad you found the cookies," Trish said. "I didn't think to offer."

Sam nodded, vaguely aware he held a cookie. Trish refilled his cup of milk and poured one for herself.

Watching as she sat down, he cast about in his mind for something safe to say. Something non-sexual. "I like milk and cookies sometimes."

She smiled. "With all the Thanksgiving food I prepared

this week, I shut off my conscience. Tyler figures store-bought cookies are a treat, anyway, since I tend to sneak healthy ingredients into mine."

"You bake cookies?" He couldn't believe it. His mother had always claimed she didn't have time to bake. "That's surprising, what with you owning a store and all."

Trish shrugged. "Everyone has twenty-four hours in her day. You just have to decide what's important and do it."

Which summed up his mother's priorities in a nutshell. Maybe Trish was different from his mother, not as obsessed with her career. The possibility pleased him, for her son's sake, of course. "Is your son at Jenny's?"

Her brow furrowed. "Weren't you just there?"

"No, I had the shop vac at my place, sweeping up some wood splinters and plaster. I have one, but..." He stopped, not wanting to mention his business. She might recognize the company name. If she wanted a rich husband, it wouldn't take long for her to zero in on him.

"Oh, gosh, I'm sorry. Jenny didn't tell me you were already borrowing the vac. I could have mopped it instead. It would have just taken longer."

"I was ready for a break." He grinned wryly. "Besides, my place is so rough, a little delay like this won't make any difference."

Trish stilled, her breathing so silent Sam was tempted to check for a pulse. Touch her and see if she was warm. Stroke her soft inner wrist and–

He cleared his throat. "Did you ship your son over to Jen's so you could fix the bathroom?"

She grimaced. "Not exactly. I'd planned to put up my outdoor Christmas lights. Tyler gets bored with it, and it's hard to watch him from the top of a ladder. It was only after I got back from dropping off Ty that I heard the toilet still running and found the mess."

"What makes me think Tyler's responsible?"

"You're a good guesser. Or maybe you had a similar misspent childhood?"

Sam lifted his mouth into a smile, hoping Trish would think it genuine. "Never. I was too scared of my mother to stop up the toilet."

She stared. Sam braced himself for the questions his comment would bring.

Trish took a sip of her milk. "He flushed his toy horse."

Sam shook his head, his relief at the change of subject overrun by his concern for a child he'd never met. His mother would have been chillingly disapproving as only she could be. He almost shuddered. "What will happen to him?"

"Horsey gets put on the shelf for a week."

Sam laughed. "You're punishing the toy? I meant, what

happens to Tyler?"

"That's it. He loves that stupid plastic horse. It goes to bed with him. And to meal time. And, I suspect, even to school. So, for one week, Horsey will sit there."

Sam swiveled to see where she pointed at the pass-through opening from the kitchen to the living room. Glancing around, Sam realized the ledge could be seen from most of the rooms in the front of the small house. Tyler would go by it twenty times a day. "Poor kid."

"I know. I'm not sure if I can stand to watch him look at Horsey for the next sixteen meals." She groaned. "I think I'll just spank him and get it over with."

"Why do you think he did it? To see what would happen, if the horse would go down the drain?"

"No, I'm certain Horsey slipped out of his hands. Ty would never experiment with this particular toy."

"Then why punish him?"

Trish looked Sam in the eye. "Because he didn't tell me. Honesty is the most important thing I can teach him. You can't have trust without honesty. Without trust..." She shrugged. "It's something I feel strongly about."

"So I see." Sam dunked a cookie, watching the bubbles pop in his milk.

A silence fell between them.

Her desire to raise an honest child stirred something in him. She was willing to live through the boy's anguish to teach him a valuable lesson. His own mother would have spanked him and then not spoken until she forgot she was angry. He couldn't decide if this was a better method of parenting.

Feeling unsettled–he didn't have to worry about the child's upbringing, after all–Sam wanted to do something nice for the boy. He couldn't talk Trish out of the punishment, but there was something else he could do.

"You probably know Jenny asked me to play Santa for your son. I thought I had plans, but I don't. Jenny's having supper later on the twenty-fourth and I'd promised not to miss it," he improvised. "But I can work in this visit before or after."

"I hate to ask you for a favor since we've only just met."

"We're both friends of Bart and Jenny's. That entitles you."

"Okay then." She inhaled deeply. "I'd like to hire you to play Santa Claus. Some of the kids at school have older brothers and sisters who've clued them in, and they've told Tyler." She tucked a strand of her silky red-gold hair behind her ear. "Nick might have questions, too, since he helped Tyler write the letter."

"A letter to Santa?"

Trish retrieved a piece of off-white, wide-ruled paper from her purse and pushed it toward him. He remembered hunching over a tablet with paper like this when he'd been learning the alphabet. He reached for the letter, surprised when Trish snatched back her hand.

Sam frowned. Shrugging off her cold reaction, he picked up the letter and read it. The boy's phrasing tickled him. *If you're you.* Sam chuckled. He loved the reminder about the bike, just in case Santa existed. Tyler sounded like a smart kid, covering all his options. The letter was too full of hope to go unanswered. "I'll do it."

"Thank you. This means a great deal to me. I don't know how much to offer you, but whatever you think is fair will be fine."

"That's not necessary. Jenny will let me borrow the costume from her school so there won't be any cost involved. I'm playing Santa for them this year." He leaned forward, unable to resist teasing her. He winked and dropped his voice. "So you'll be getting a man of experience."

Trish jerked back and her face flamed. Sam tried to keep his expression innocent.

"Yes. Well. That's good." She cleared her throat. "Tyler wants Santa to wake him up. You'd have to come after Ty's in bed."

"No problem. What time does he go to bed?"

"Since it's Christmas Eve, he'll be wound up. Maybe you

should wait until ten. Or eleven." She smiled, softening at the mention of her son, and Sam stiffened against her allure. "He sleeps as soundly as a hibernating bear. If you speak to him quietly, he'll probably go right back to sleep."

"That's fine."

"I appreciate you doing this."

Sam hesitated, not wanting to be a macho jerk and insult her abilities, but also not wanting her to have to struggle with something he could do easily. It couldn't hurt to ask. "Do you need any help putting his bike together?"

"I haven't taken the training wheels off his little bike yet." She shifted self-consciously. "I suppose I'm overprotective. Tyler must have decided to go over my head to a higher authority."

"Santa Claus?"

Trish nodded with a rueful smile.

"Smart kid. He knows you can't very well refuse to let him ride a bike Santa brings."

"I haven't even bought a bike yet. He didn't ask *me* for one, so I only discovered he wanted a big-boy bike when I found this letter." She sighed.

"If you do need help with the assembly, let me know."

"Having you play Santa takes a load off my mind. He's already had so much to deal with, not having a father."

"I'm glad to do it." Sam wanted to reassure this young

boy, even though his mother confounded him. One moment she was warm and grateful, the next she pulled her hand away like he was a leper.

"I do want to pay you, though."

"Don't be ridiculous. Jenny would skin me alive or worse, refuse to feed me." Sam laughed at the idea.

Trish's smile tightened at the corners.

He ate his cookie slowly, thinking. He should load up the shop vac and get back to work at his place. God knew, there was enough to do there, but he didn't want to leave. "So," he said, "what do you say we get those Christmas lights hung?"

*

Later, Trish couldn't recall how it happened. One minute, she was sitting in the kitchen, protesting against Sam's helping her; the next, she was showing him where she stored the ladder. Her arguing that he had too much to do fell on deaf ears. Sam obviously wanted to help. Trish wondered if he was as motivated to fix his own house and get moved out of Jenny and Bart's. Or maybe he enjoyed having Jenny cook all his meals. Jenny probably threw in his clothes when doing laundry without making a big deal out of it. And it wasn't a big deal, not if Sam appreciated it.

Trish stood on the porch as Sam walked around the corner of the house, her aluminum extension ladder balanced on his broad shoulder. She looked him over, all six foot plus of him. Sam had left his jacket in her kitchen in honor of the warm day, which made it easier for her to appreciate his body. His broad chest supported his shoulders. Although it was difficult to judge what lay under his tan cable-knit sweater, Trish supposed he didn't have an extra inch of fat on him. Lean from hunger or lean from the hard, physical work of a carpenter?

Sam stopped at the bottom of the steps. The wind ruffled his hair, lifting thick layers like a lover's caress. She glanced down into his eyes. Twinkling blue.

Taking an abrupt step back, Trish heard the porch creak under her weight.

"Whoa, there." Sam reached out with his free hand and grabbed her forearm. The heat of his touch seared through her thin cotton sweater. "That porch is none too solid. Those boards ought to be replaced." He propped the ladder below the gutters. "Now, how about you direct and I hang?"

Trish only nodded. He mentioned the hard winter to come with concern for her safety but not a word about his own circumstances. She stared at him, puzzled.

He cleared his throat. "We'll need the lights."

Trish blushed at being caught daydreaming and scurried inside, only to find Sam right on her heels. She led him to the laundry area in the basement and pointed at boxes, which he reached without the stepladder she always needed.

"You're very organized." Sam gestured at the boxes lined up on her homemade shelves. A label on each box indicated its contents. "Halloween, Thanksgiving, Easter. Summer? What's in there?"

"Sandbox toys, pool stuff." Trish shifted her shoulders into a shrug. "I have to be organized to be a quilter. I guess I'm compulsive, huh?"

"No, it's great. I never know where I've stored things. I'm always finding a 'lost' box of Christmas lights when I put my decorations back away in January."

Trish relaxed her expression into something non-committal. She didn't want Sam to ask questions. How could she explain her confusion? Why would he put up Christmas lights on a rundown house? How could he afford the electric bill?

"I have to ask you something," Sam said.

Trish looked up to find his eyes lit with humor. An adorable grin showed off his deep dimples. Trish cleared her throat. "What?"

"Do you really have six boxes of lights?"

Trish saw the box he held marked, "Xmas Lights–OD–1/6." She laughed and tapped the letters. "These are just the outdoor lights for the house and the trees." She took the box from him, steadfastly ignoring the tingle in her fingers as they brushed his. She nodded at the top shelf. "The other five are up there. Beside those are the indoor decorations. I keep the large Nativity figures for the yard in the attic over the garage."

She turned and walked toward the door out of the utility room, stopping to flash a smile over her shoulder at a stunned Sam. He laughed, a deep rumbling sound that filled her with warmth.

As she crossed the porch and set down the box, Trish recalled Sam's advice about the porch boards. She went over and stepped on the one by her steps. It bent under her weight.

Sam bumped open the screen door with the two boxes he carried. He placed them at the far end of the porch, then walked out to the middle of her yard and turned around. His hands rested on his lean hips as he studied her house.

After a few moments, Trish's curiosity got the better of her. She strolled over and stood beside him, trying to figure out what he studied with such a pensive expression.

The house was a simple ranch-style, built in the early 1970s. When they remodeled, Duke had chosen light brown aluminum siding to go with the darker brown brick facade. The house had always reminded Trish of an acorn. She used to joke that they lived in a nut house, but Duke hadn't appreciated her humor. She loved the house and had meant the joke with affection. The house was small and cute and brown.

She tried to see it through Sam's eyes. A long wooden porch stretched across two-thirds of the front. Three beige columns held up the overhang. Evergreen shrubs lined up under the bedroom windows to the right. The large maple tree that shaded the house in the summer now decorated the yard with red and gold leaves.

She peered at Sam. "What are you looking at?"

He glanced down at her from the corner of his eye. "I'm wondering where you hang six boxes of lights. I want to make sure I didn't just volunteer to decorate a five story house."

Trish laughed and crossed back to the porch. He came over to her, flashing a devastating smile that made her skin tingle. Leaning forward, he stepped on the faulty board, which protested under his weight. "Yep, ought to be replaced."

Trish watched Sam turn and go back inside, presumably for more boxes. She shook her head at herself. A crazy idea banged around in her brain. She shouldn't even consider it. She definitely wouldn't say it out loud.

But as Sam stood on the ladder above her, patiently hanging the lights where she indicated, Trish couldn't get the idea to go away. She wandered back to the porch, lightly bouncing on the board, worrying it like a loose tooth. She went over to the bottom of the ladder and looked up. "Sam."

He glanced down at her. "Yeah?"

"Those boards need to be replaced before bad weather, right?"

Sam nodded. "Long-term forecast predicts lots of snow and bitter cold temperatures. You won't get much snow built up under the porch there, but it'll get wet. Even if the boards stay dry, they're still dangerous. You or your boy might get hurt."

Trish nodded, chewing her lip. Exhaling a deep breath, she let go of her reservations along with her common sense. "Would you like the job?"

He cocked his head in question.

"I would pay you, of course." Trish worried he was embarrassed and rushed on. "There are boards in the basement, but I might have to get some new paint. And there are a few other things around the house you could do for me. If you have time."

Heat rose from her collar. Trying not to embarrass Sam about needing money or being out of work, she'd only fumbled and made things worse. Even now he was coming down the ladder, probably ready to walk off with his hurt pride.

She looked away. "If you don't want to, don't worry about it."

"I didn't say I didn't want to."

Trish glanced at him.

Sam's gaze searched her face. "What other things need to

be done?"

Maybe he did want to work, after all. "I need to replace the kitchen sink. It leaks and can't be patched again. Also, I bought some ceiling fans on sale after summer. Those aren't urgent, but as long as you're doing the rest..."

When he didn't answer right away, Trish figured she'd been mistaken. Sam wasn't interested in work. He just planned to take advantage of Jenny and Bart's generosity. She should be relieved to find out now, before she grew any more attracted to his charm or his humor. Or his body. She'd wanted to help him out, but she sure didn't need him around to entice her away from her common sense.

Trish smiled a little, letting him off the hook, sure he'd refuse, anyway. She regretted mentioning it. "I guess you're busy, fixing your own place and all."

"I could make time."

Trish shoved her hands in her jeans pockets. Was he accepting? Or was he just stuck in an awkward situation, having friends in common?

"I'm hosting my family's Christmas dinner," she explained, "and I don't want them to get injured. I have so many quilt orders to fill, I don't know where I'll find the time. I'd like to fix the sink and the porch before then."

Realizing she'd definitely put him on the spot, she smiled

brightly. "But don't give it another thought. I can cope with the sink till after Christmas. And I'll find time for the boards. It's no big deal." She patted his arm and headed for the porch.

"I'll do it."

Trish had taken only two steps before he spoke. She whirled back toward him with a huge smile. "Really?"

"Sure. I can do all of it."

"Oh, good. I know you're busy at your house. I really appreciate this. And the money will come in handy for your own repairs."

Trish flushed as his brows rose. She waved her hand in dismissal. "We can all use money sometimes, especially when we're fixing up a house." When he continued to stare at her, she shrugged. "Look. We might as well clear the air. Jenny told me about...well, about your circumstances."

"My circumstances?"

Trish fixed her gaze on a bunch of maple leaves blown beneath a shrub. "About you not working right now and living with them because of your house being in such bad shape. And she's worried you won't have heat."

CHAPTER THREE

Sam's mouth dropped open in disbelief.

"I'm sorry if you didn't want me to know, but I do." Crossing the yard quickly toward the house, Trish called out over her shoulder, "I'm going to make some hot chocolate. Come in when you want yours."

He stared after her retreating figure. What in the world had Jenny told her?

He ran Trish's comments through his mind again, trying to make sense of them. Her initial remark confused him. What circumstances?

Something about her mention of the slow construction season and him living with the McIntires while he rehabbed a house for a profitable resell didn't sound right. Over the holidays, he usually took an extended vacation and let his crew work on the indoor jobs. He got a break, and he usually didn't have to lay off anyone. Maybe Trish just didn't understand how his business worked.

What else had she said? That Jenny thought he'd turn off his heat? No decent contractor would freeze a building's pipes. He knew under what circumstances he could do that safely.

Sam couldn't pinpoint the problem. What Trish said made him uneasy, but after replaying her words in his mind, he couldn't figure out why. Everything she'd said was true. He wasn't working, and he was living with Bart and Jenny right now. Maybe she had assumed it was because his house was in such bad shape, and that was partly true. This new acquisition would be a doozy to fix and flip for a profit in this economy. Mostly he was living with them because Jen had asked him to stay over the holidays. Trish's worry that he wouldn't have heat must have originated with Jenny, who didn't understand his business either. Shrugging off his disquiet, he climbed the ladder to finish decorating the front of the house.

The lure of hot chocolate brought him in thirty minutes later. He found Trish sitting at the kitchen table with some sewing in her lap. She jumped up when she saw him and warmed his mug in the microwave.

She set it in front of him and sat back down in the chair to his left. Sam added a handful of miniature marshmallows from the bowl on the table. The rich smell of chocolate made his stomach growl. He took a cautious sip, grateful for the warmth, even though it was in the mid- fifties outside.

"This tastes like real hot chocolate." Sam noticed Trish's

surprise. "You know, the kind with milk."

She eyed him as though he was loony. "I made it with milk." Trish resumed sewing with a little smile.

Sam sipped his chocolate. *She makes real hot chocolate. Bakes cookies. Sews.* He grinned. Trish sounded too good to be true, the ideal housewife.

Housewife? Ideal? Sam clamped a vise on his fantasies. Trish was a career-woman, not a homebody. She owned a store. He'd learned from his mother the single-minded dedication a woman needed to succeed in the business world, let alone one who ran her own business.

"What are you making?" He indicated the sewing she held with a nod of his head.

"I'm quilting a vest, a custom-order for Christmas."

Sam eyed the pink and maroon colors and cocked his brow. "Is that really for Christmas?"

"My customer picked the design and the colors. She considers this to be the ultimate in Victorian style, much more chic than traditional red and green." Trish grinned. "Who am I to argue? She's the one who'll have to wear mauve Christmas trees and burgundy snowflakes to her party."

"Do you get a lot of custom orders?"

Trish nodded. "Most are for quilts, since that's a bigger project than most women want to tackle. I have three more quilt orders left to do for Christmas and one for a wedding gift on New Year's Eve. I also have this vest to finish and a few pillows."

Sam blinked. "You have four quilts to do in four weeks? Isn't that a lot? I mean, I don't know anything about sewing, past replacing a lost button, but shouldn't you have started sooner?"

Trish's tinkling laughter filled the room. Her hand came up to cover her mouth. Bright green eyes glinted at him above her fingers. "Sorry, I don't mean to laugh. Of course, it would be too late. I'd never finish if I just started now."

"I'll help you. I'll do all the house repairs. It's no wonder you can't find any time to do them."

Sam liked the way Trish looked at him, even if he couldn't figure out why she looked like that, so soft and warm. He cleared his throat.

"You're a very sweet man, Sam Carrow. I appreciate your offer." Trish smiled at him as she laid her hand on his forearm. She withdrew it way too soon to suit him. "I began work on each quilt as soon as it was ordered. They're in various stages of completion, but I'll get them done long before the dates I promised."

"Oh."

"But I do still need you to fix the house."

"That I can do."

"I'll be relieved to get it off my mind. And while I'm thinking about it–" Trish rose and walked toward the doorway. "I have some home repair books you might want to study."

Sam stared at the empty doorway. *Home repair books? For a building contractor?*

The women he'd dated would have called a professional–like him–for repairs. They'd snap their fingers, expecting the world to jump to do their bidding. They'd never have bought a book and taught themselves.

When she returned carrying four books, Sam couldn't help but be curious. He checked out the titles as she placed them on the table, one by one. *Every Woman's Guide to Ceiling Fans. How to Patch Almost Anything. Paint Like a Pro.*

"I thought you could use this one for the front porch." Trish set down *Build Your Deck This Weekend.* "I haven't gotten around to building a deck yet. And my plumbing book is in the basement bathroom, of course."

"Of course." Now he knew how she'd retrieved Tyler's toy horse. She'd just read a book and plunged in. Sam grinned at his pun and looked at her in wonder.

"What?" She slid back into her seat.

He shook his head. A 50s housewife who could snake a drain? A career woman who thought of something other than work? "You fix all this yourself? I'm impressed."

Trish shrugged and stirred her chocolate. "A book is much cheaper than a plumber. Unless I find a rich husband or win the Lotto, I can't afford to hire anyone else." Her gaze shot to his. "I'll pay you for what you're doing, of course. I didn't mean I couldn't afford to."

A solid block pressed against his chest. Her comment about a rich husband cemented his conviction to avoid her. He'd tell her the truth, then send over a laborer for these projects. His debt to Bart and Jenny would be repaid, and he wouldn't have to be around Trish. He wouldn't need to see her again, other than Christmas Eve. "I won't need those books."

"Really?" She stopped stirring to glance up at him. "Have you had to do these things on your own house?"

"I've done most of it. The place was a wreck when I bought it. But I meant–"

The ringing of the telephone cut off his words. Sam growled under his breath. Maybe he shouldn't tell her about his company. Why give her cause to pursue him?

"Excuse me." Trish walked over and answered the phone. The extra-long cord allowed her to reach back to the table to get her mug. Sam heard her laugh and tell Jenny it was safe for Tyler to come home for dinner, and she would come get him now. He watched as she sipped her chocolate, then wrinkled her nose and set it in the sink. Her tongue darted out and licked the fuzz of cold chocolate from her upper lip.

Desire burned in his gut, churning against that hard place in his chest. She chuckled again, her eyes full of laughter. Trish seemed oblivious to his attraction to her. He watched her progress as she rinsed out her mug, came over and peeked in his, raised her light golden eyebrows, then at his nod, snatched up his mug to rinse as well. She flitted around the tiny kitchen during the conversation, tidying up here, then gliding by to pop a marshmallow in her mouth before straightening a pile of cookbooks over there.

Obviously, Trish had no idea how to relax. He'd love to teach her. Against his better instincts, he wanted to get closer to her, like a mouse drawn to the cheese in a trap. He shook his head at himself. Whatever she did to him, he'd deserve it. Part of him almost didn't care.

"Gotta go," she said after about three minutes. "Sam's still here. Um-hmm, I'm sure you forgot he had the shop vac." Trish flashed him a bright smile. "It's been great having him here today. He even hung my Christmas lights." Her face flamed before she whirled away to stand with her back to him. "Don't be ridiculous," she hissed. "I'll be over in a few minutes to get Tyler. Good-bye." She hung up the wall phone but didn't turn around.

"What did Jenny say?"

Trish glanced over her shoulder at him. "What?"

"What'd she say to make you blush?"

Her face turned scarlet once more. Sam suppressed his grin. As a redhead, Trish sure couldn't hide when she was embarrassed. "Did she say something about me?"

Trish leaned her back against the wall. "The whole conversation was about you. Jenny wanted to know when you could try on the Santa suit. She wants to get it out and see if it needs to go to the cleaners."

"Why would she ask you about my schedule?"

Trish shrugged even as the color crept back into her face. "How should I know? Jenny and I have been friends for a couple of years now, but I still can't figure out how her mind works."

Sam nodded, but he didn't buy it. Jenny was doing some matchmaking, obviously. Trish's blushes could indicate anything from interest in him to horror at the mere idea of them being together. Despite his reservations, he couldn't help but be curious about her feelings.

*

Trish followed Sam as he carried the shop vac up the stairs and out to a pickup truck. Falling twilight hid the lettering on the black doors. A company truck? Who did he borrow it from?

The tailgate slammed shut. Sam leaned back against the truck, propping his elbows on top of the tailgate and hooking his boot heel on the bumper. Trish stepped away. He studied her with his head tilted to the side, as if trying to work through a problem or phrase a question.

Trish waited. Sam was easy to watch. His indolent pose against the truck was sexier than anything she'd ever seen. She wistfully envisioned Sam with a black cowboy hat, chewing a length of hay, and looking at her in just that way. As though the problem he was working through was how to toss her on a bale of hay and have his wicked way with her. As though the question he was trying to phrase was, *Your place or mine?*

Trish grinned. They were already at her place.

"Guess we'd better get going." Sam pushed himself away from the truck.

Trish hid her confusion behind a smile. She'd seen the flash of interest in his eyes.

"Jenny might not hold dinner for us," he said.

Reality stabbed her like a sharp needle. She didn't need his kisses to make her lose her head. Sam was a user, and she'd be better off remembering that. Getting involved with him was the last thing she should want. She just seemed to have trouble remembering that when he was around. "I'm not staying for dinner," she said. "I'm just going to pick up Tyler."

"Jenny will talk you into staying."

"Jenny will try," she acknowledged with a dip of her

head, "but I don't think it's a good idea."

"Why not?" Sam stepped toward her, close enough for Trish to see the question on his tanned face.

She wanted to see his eyes more clearly. Had they really darkened when he stepped nearer? Was he affected by her, after all? Was she crazy to be attracted to him? "I don't think we should spend too much time together."

Sam's head jerked back. He considered her for a moment, then stepped even closer. "Why not?"

Trish tried not to squirm. She wanted to shout at him. *Because you're living off other people and are happy to do it. Because you lack ambition, and I've had that once. Because you're sexy as sin, and you're scaring me to death.*

Her heart lodged in her throat, making it impossible to either breathe or speak. She trained her gaze on the collar of Sam's sweater. Casting in her mind, she blurted, "I don't want Tyler to get to know you."

Even in the faint light, she saw Sam stiffen.

"I mean...because of the Santa thing. If we spend too much time together, he'll recognize you when you come over on Christmas Eve. His Christmas will be ruined."

Sam nodded, not taking his gaze off hers. He didn't speak for a long moment, making Trish wonder if he doubted her.

"So," Sam said finally, "I guess I'll be coming over to fix

the house when Tyler's not around."

Trish stilled, every muscle frozen as she bumped against the corner she'd just backed herself into. She was almost positive Sam's eyes twinkled in the fading light.

*

Sam followed Trish's taillights back to Bart and Jenny's, pretty sure now of Trish's interest in him. But why the resistance?

Why wouldn't Trish want to get to know him? Was it this crazy idea she had of him being penniless? He'd hung five strings of lights before he'd finally figured that out. All those things she'd said about his house being a wreck and his being out of work and living with Bart's family. Once he'd stopped thinking how true it all was, he heard what Trish hadn't said, the polite gaps she thought he'd understand. How she'd gotten this idea was a mystery.

What he planned to do about it was a dilemma.

Sam knew he ought to set her straight. Be honorable. If he did it now, she wouldn't be too embarrassed about a simple misunderstanding.

On the other hand...

He might enjoy not being chased for his money. Women put themselves in his path once they found out about his healthy bank account. Sherry had been the last in a stream of greedy women. He scowled, remembering the other women who'd mostly wanted his money or the things his money could buy them.

Judging Trish by the actions of other women was unfair, but experience had taught him to be wary. Jenny had said Trish wanted a rich husband. Hell, Trish had confirmed it a few minutes before in her kitchen.

Sam grinned at the irony. For years, he'd concentrated on building his business and had dated women who understood he wanted no strings. Now that it was time to start a family, he didn't know a woman he would want to marry. Trish's devotion to her career made her an unlikely candidate.

A replay of Trish tucking her hair behind her ear flashed through his mind. Someone ought to tell her what a dead giveaway that gesture was. She wanted him, even though she believed he was destitute.

An insane desire to shove her snobbery back in her face rushed through him.

He'd love to tell her he was just rehabbing that wreck of a house for resell, and it wasn't about to be condemned. He'd tell her he owned the construction company and had built some of the finest, most expensive subdivisions in three counties. He'd tell her he was waiting to build his own house until he had a wife to make it feel more like a home than an empty shell.

Then he'd tell her she'd missed her chance for a rich husband.

Sam sighed and ran a hand through his hair.

Hurting Trish wouldn't help him get over Sherry's defection. Playing "poor Sam" would shield him from her schemes. He wished he understood his compulsion to help her out, but until he got over it, he'd just remember his role and keep her at arm's length.

*

"Tyler, we've been over this," Trish said to her son the next morning. "Horsey has to stay on that shelf for the whole week."

"I was just going to take him to church."

"No."

"But it was an accident. I didn't mean to drop Horsey in the potty. He just slipped."

Trish knelt down, careful not to snag her hose on the chipped linoleum, and gently grasped Tyler's hands. She brushed a lock of white-blond hair off his forehead, enjoying the feel of the silky strands sliding through her fingers. Clear green eyes proclaimed his innocence and made her heart ache with love.

"I believe it was an accident, Ty. But you didn't tell me when Horsey fell in. You need to learn to tell me the truth, no matter what."

"You would have been mad at me." His eyes filled with tears. "I couldn't get Horsey out, and I couldn't make the water stop running."

Trish clutched him to her and kissed the side of his head. She had to swallow tears of her own. She felt humbled, as always, to think of having such great importance in her son's life. She knew he clung to her and courted her approval more than most five-year-olds because he lacked a father. It downright terrified her sometimes.

"I wouldn't have been happy about it, honey," she said, "but I wouldn't have been mad. Being honest helps you grow into a good person. Did you feel good inside when you didn't tell me Horsey got stuck in the toilet?"

Tyler shook his head.

"That's the virtue, the best part, of telling the truth. It makes you feel good. If you'd told me right away, there wouldn't have been such a mess for me to clean up." She sat back on her heels, holding his hands.

Ty stood silent for a moment. Trish could almost see him working through it. "If I'd told you right away, would Horsey have to be on the shelf?"

"No, not after you explained it was an accident."

"Oh." Tyler hung his head. "But now it's too late?"

Trish winced, feeling like Attila the Mom. She wanted to

give in, although it would be a disastrous mistake. "I want you to remember to be honest with me, even if you think you might get in trouble. Tyler, I'm always going to love you. Being angry at you won't change that."

"But, Mom, Horsey has to come with us." Tyler raised soulful eyes. "He's never missed church before."

"No, Tyler," Trish said firmly, rising and brushing down her skirt.

"Okay," Tyler said with a dark scowl. "But God's not going to like it." He spun and rushed from the room.

The telephone rang, saving Trish from finding an answer. *Kids.* She smiled as she picked up the receiver. Trish heard her mother-in-law's voice and glanced at the kitchen wall clock. "Hello, Miriam. We were just on our way out to church."

"I won't keep you, dear. I understand you have so little time to talk to me."

Trish rolled her eyes. So, it was Miriam the Martyr calling this morning.

"What I was calling about, dear, is Christmas. We see so little of Tyler these days. We were hoping he could spend some time with us over his school vacation. Maybe he can stay overnight here."

"That sounds lovely, Miriam. Ty will like that. When did you have in mind?" Trish strolled over to her wall calendar.

She noted the date of Jenny and Bart's party and suggested that night to Miriam.

"Oh, dear, no. That's almost an entire week before Christmas. I hoped we could watch little Tyler open his presents this year. He'll never be five again. It's such a precious stage in a child's life."

Trish ground her teeth together. Ty opened presents with his grandparents every year. She took a deep breath, determined not to give in to Miriam's manipulation.

"I was hoping, dear, that Tyler could spend Christmas Eve with us. We could have a nice breakfast and bring him home after church."

Trish grasped the phone, speechless. Miriam wanted Tyler to spend Christmas Eve and Christmas morning with them, rather than with his own mother?

"That's impossible." Trish heard Miriam gasp and wished she'd been more tactful. Unfortunately, she didn't feel tactful. "I'm sorry, Miriam, but Ty has to be home to open his presents from Santa Claus. It's especially important this year."

"We could tell him Santa brought his presents to our house. Lots of children who travel from their homes to visit relatives during the holidays are told that."

"Not this year. I want Tyler to open his presents here."

Trish waited. Miriam's heavy silence sent a shiver up her neck. She could feel the older woman's displeasure.

"Trish, dear, Tyler will understand. My friend, Lucille, tells that to her granddaughter, Rose, and Rose believes it."

Another chill chased the first. Lucille had won full custody of Rose last year, tearing the child away from her "unfit" mother, Lucille's ex-daughter-in-law. For Miriam to mention Lucille felt ominous, like a gunshot fired over her head, just to make her duck.

Trish swallowed, her throat dry. "I'm sorry, Miriam. We'll have to work out another date for Tyler to stay overnight. Now, if you'll excuse me, I have to go to church."

She hung up and pressed a hand to her churning stomach. Miriam didn't like being told no. What maneuver would she try next, and how could Trish keep Tyler from getting hurt?

CHAPTER FOUR

"So, how's it going with the handyman?"

Trish glanced at her assistant, Candy Clark, the next Wednesday. They sat in the back office of the fabric shop, where Trish prepared the end of the month report for the accountant and Candy ordered supplies. The store didn't open for another hour, and she enjoyed this quiet time discussing business and catching up on each other's lives.

Trish paused with her fingers over the calculator. Candy had been with her since she opened Fancy Fabrics three years earlier. Candy had traded her skills as an eighteen-year-old babysitter to two-year-old Tyler in return for learning to operate the cash register and handle different business procedures. Both women had considered the deal short-term.

They'd been through the early struggles together, becoming even closer friends as the store triumphed into steady black ink after only ten months. They'd shared a lot, but this... This was Sam. Trish wasn't sure how she felt, let alone what she wanted to share. "He's doing some work for me tomorrow."

Candy wiggled her thin eyebrows in a leer. "So, is he 'handy around the house?'"

Trish laughed lightly. "That's all you pregnant women ever think about."

"Wouldn't hurt you to think about it, either."

Trish scowled and resumed her calculations. It was the beginning of December, a surprisingly busy season. She didn't have time for nonsense.

"Come on, Trish. Sam sounds like a dream. Don't tell me you haven't at least thought about having a closer relationship with him."

"Okay," she said without looking up, "I won't tell you."

"Have you?" Candy toddled over as fast as she could, being seven months along, and perched on Trish's desk.

Trish leaned back with a sigh and rubbed her temples. "Getting involved with Sam would be crazy."

"You have thought about it!" Candy's face lit with excitement. Her blue eyes glowed, her chubby cheeks became more radiant and even her smile beamed brighter.

Trish felt tired just looking at her. "Don't fall off the desk. I wouldn't want Max forbidding you to work here because it endangers the baby."

"Max doesn't forbid me to do anything."

Trish smiled wryly. "Because he's afraid of you."

"Because he adores me. Besides, we've been married two years now." Candy giggled. "He already knows giving me orders doesn't do any good."

Trish shook her head, smiling. Candy was a five foot tall, chubby blonde bubble. She was irresistibly charming and fun. And so very young. Some days, Trish couldn't even remember feeling that young, although she'd only been twenty-five when she had Tyler.

"Don't change the subject." Candy shook a finger at Trish. "We were talking about you and Sam getting together."

"No, we weren't. We were talking about how crazy and impossible the idea is."

"Is he married?" When Trish shook her head no, Candy sighed loudly. "Then it's possible. You're definitely available."

"Gee, thanks."

"So, what's stopping you? Is it because he's poor?"

"Of course not."

Candy cocked a brow at her vehemence. "Are you sure?"

Trish swallowed a sense of betrayal. It was a reasonable question, one the irrepressible Candy would naturally ask. After a moment's honest consideration, Trish shook her head. "It's because being poor doesn't seem to matter to him."

Candy tilted her head and frowned. "What do you

mean?"

Trish shrugged. "I don't understand him. He doesn't have a job or even look for one."

"He's doing this work for you."

"But this just fell in his lap."

After a moment, Candy said, "Are you resisting him because he reminds you of Duke?"

Trish jerked back instinctively. Rarely did anyone mention her deceased husband, and then only in glowing terms. She thought she'd overcome her tendency to defend Duke, but it kicked in on reflex. "They're nothing alike."

"No? You've told me Duke lacked ambition. That he was perfectly content working on the line at the car factory."

Trish felt the blood drain from her face. No one ever mentioned the car factory where Duke had lost his life. She would never forget the sight of Duke's mangled body after it had been cut free from the machinery.

"You said," Candy went on, "no matter how much you encouraged him, Duke turned down all of the supervisory positions they offered him."

Trish nodded, unable to speak.

"He always talked about quitting, but never about what else he might want to do. Isn't that why you had to put your dream for this store on hold? For the security your management job provided?"

Trish sat, simply staring at Candy, unable to reply. She'd loved Duke, but she hadn't been blind to his faults. Candy's assessment of him was right on target, formed over the years from tidbits Trish had shared. Obviously, she'd been more honest than she thought.

Sam showed even less ambition and self-respect. She feared he'd lie to her, as Duke had, to make up for that lack.

Candy returned to her own desk. Trish could only think about Sam and Duke. They were a lot alike, fun and laid-back to a fault. She'd loved the wrong man once–that was enough for a lifetime.

"Maybe I'm wrong," Candy said quietly.

Trish swiveled her chair toward Candy's desk. Candy stared at the pen she rolled between her fingers, not meeting her gaze. "Maybe you should talk to Jenny about Sam. I don't know him. She does."

Trish's laugh sounded as hollow as she felt. "Jenny would hang me out to dry. Sam is as dear to her as I am, maybe more so. I could never get an unbiased opinion from her." Trish tucked her hair behind her ear, releasing a deep sigh. "Besides, I'm afraid you're right. Sam does remind me of Duke."

They sat for a few minutes without speaking. Trish could tell by her hunched posture that Candy regretted her candor.

Trying to lighten the mood, she said, "Don't frown. You'll give the baby colic."

Candy looked up quickly, as susceptible to old wives' tales as any first-time mom.

Trish grinned. "Gotcha."

Candy grinned in return. "Very funny. Just do me a favor and think about this. If Sam was rich, with a steady job and he was a classic workaholic, would you want him then?"

Trish met Candy's gaze straight on. "I'm trying not to want him now."

As Candy nodded her encouragement, Trish swung back to her own desk. "Because I'm not going to have him."

Throughout the night she tossed and turned–tossing out ideas of her and Sam together, turning back to them as she cuddled her pillow in her huge, lonely bed.

During breakfast, Trish held fast to her belief that she should be a friend to Sam without getting romantically involved with him. Limiting their relationship would leave her with only wistful dreams of what might have been. If they acted on their mutual attraction, it might be heavenly for a while, but the eventual break-up would devastate her. Instinctively, she shied away from giving another man that much power over her life.

But, Lord, was she tempted to reach for heaven, at least

for a while.

She drove Tyler to school, watching his tow-headed figure race into the building with his buddies. Sam would have a disastrous influence on her son. How could Tyler acquire a decent, middle-class work ethic if the man his mother dated lacked one? She arrived home ashamed of herself, but knowing her decision to avoid an emotional entanglement with Sam was the best choice for her and Tyler.

Then the doorbell rang, and anticipation surged through Trish. She raced to the door, as eager to be with Sam as Tyler had been to be with his friends. She paused before the mirror to push her hair into place.

Catching sight of the excited glow in her eyes, she laughed mockingly. Who was she kidding? She didn't want to stop at friendship. She wanted to pursue all the possibilities of this relationship. No limits, no boundaries. Just this wondrous, *alive* feeling he created in her.

Trish swung open the door with a huge smile.

Sam looked magnificent. His navy blue eyes glowed, letting her know how happy he was to see her even before he smiled. His sheepskin coat added bulk to his already wide shoulders. Worn jeans fit snugly across his thighs. His dark blond hair had been tousled by the breeze. He looked warm and cuddly.

Trish stepped back to let him enter. "Good morning."

"Appears to be." Sam set down a carpenter's box full of tools and rubbed his hands together. "It's brisk right now, but it's supposed to be sunny later. I'd like to start on the porch boards. I've been worrying all week about you getting hurt."

He was getting straight to work. She should be relieved. So why did she want him to hang around talking to her instead? "Would you like some coffee first?"

"No, thanks. I thought I'd measure the boards that need replacing. Did you say you have some wood I might be able to use?"

Trish nodded.

"I need to see if it's sound or if I need to make a trip to the lumber yard. I can paint this morning and nail them in place later today while it's nice."

Trish smiled, hoping she looked more enthusiastic than she felt. At this rate, he'd be done with all her house repairs in two days. It was probably for the best.

"Do you want me to cut the boards in the basement or the garage?"

"In the garage, I guess."

Sam picked up his carpenter's box, appearing eager to get started–and finished–as soon as possible.

Trish turned to lead him to the basement, careful to show no emotion. After all, why should she be upset? She'd asked him to work for her, not socialize.

Sam turned a two by twelve in his hands. "Looks sound."

She remembered a story she'd read to Tyler. A child had asked Michelangelo why he was chipping at a block of marble. The artist had told the boy, "To let out the angel trapped inside." She wondered what, if anything, Sam envisioned when he cradled the board between his rough hands. She wanted him to make something of himself the way that he would make something useful out of the hardy wood. She didn't expect perfection from him, only honest effort.

"Are you interested in carpentry as a career?" Trish asked.

Sam darted a glance at her, then studied the board he held. "I've done a lot of work with wood."

"You appear to know what to look for."

His gaze captured hers and held it for a moment, then another. "Oh, I know what I need."

Trish's scalp tingled as she fell under the spell of his husky voice.

Without breaking eye contact, Sam set the board down and stepped closer. "Strength. Integrity. The hard part is knowing the choice I make is the right one, the one that will last."

Trish's breath caught in her throat. He wasn't talking about wood. Heat radiated from him. His next step closer brought him into her personal space, but instead of tensing against the invasion, all her muscles relaxed in acceptance. She couldn't look away from his eyes, enthralled by their velvety darkness.

"I wouldn't want anyone to get hurt," Sam said in a rough whisper. He put his hands around her waist and drew her close. Just the slightest pressure from his fingertips guided her into his arms.

Trish tipped her head back and let her eyes drift closed. She gripped the fleece lapels of Sam's jacket and drew him that last necessary inch. His warm breath caressed her cheek.

Their mouths met. Sam leaned toward her, moving his lips gently over hers. It was a kiss of hello, a kiss of gentle exploration.

Trish buried her fingers in the fleece, grasping it to keep herself from flinging her arms around his neck and devouring him. She wanted to deepen the kiss.

But she didn't because this kiss was so wonderful, so new and fresh. A kiss of discovery. She discovered the scent of his skin, the softness of his lips. She discovered the delicious pleasure of his warm breath on her cheek. She rediscovered long-buried feelings of adult tenderness, and the intimacy and joy of pure need. Things she thought she'd never feel again.

So she restrained her urge to deepen the kiss and just

enjoyed what they shared. A blending of lips, a gentle pressure and a tiny nibble on her lower lip. A shiver ran down Trish's spine. He drew back. She opened her eyes, reluctant to leave the dreamy perfection of their kiss. He nuzzled his nose playfully down the short length of hers before he straightened. His smile warmed her down to her toes.

Trish released his jacket from her grip. She couldn't think of a thing to say. She lowered her gaze to his chest and smoothed his lapels, feeling the softness under her fingertips.

"Believe me, I know what I'm looking for." Sam stepped away, still smiling gently. He cleared his throat and picked up the board once again. "I'll be out on the porch."

Trish watched him walk away. When she heard him go up the stairs, she allowed herself a goofy grin. She reveled in the sheer joy of wanting a man again and knowing he was attracted to her, as well. She felt alive, in ways she hadn't since before Duke's death.

Duke. The grin dropped off her face. Trish wrapped her arms around her middle, swallowing guilt.

Wanting another man was okay, she assured herself as she walked toward her adjacent sewing room. Her husband had been dead for over four years. She hadn't been attracted to a man, let alone been tempted to start a relationship.

She was interested in Sam and wanted something with him. Not necessarily forever, but perhaps she could dip her toes into the dating pool without diving in. Test the waters with Sam. Proceed cautiously.

Since she was thinking this way, the time had obviously come for her to start dating again. Sam was a safe bet. She wouldn't risk her heart on him, knowing he was a user, but she could re-learn how to date. And have a little fun along the way.

While she was practicing with Sam, she could discover if he was as much like Duke as she feared. He appeared to be a man without drive, without ambition. A man who wandered from job to job if not actually wandering away from home. A man content to let others do for him while he glided through his days. She hoped the old adage about appearances being deceiving held true in this case.

At least Sam wasn't the habitual liar Duke had been. Duke told her only what he wanted her to hear, changing his tune as it suited his purpose. She'd never endure that again.

And Sam could kiss her senseless. A definite point in his favor.

Trish drew a deep breath and set the timer she kept on her desk. She settled at her quilt frame, remembering her frustration with Duke. She could have accepted doing without, if she'd been working at his side in a partnership of marriage, doing all she could to help provide for their family, even sacrificing her dreams to open Fancy Fabrics.

But she and Duke hadn't had a partnership.

Trish drew the thread through the layers of material and batting, wishing it had been as easy to mend the inequity in her marriage as it was to bind together a quilt. Duke had never wanted their lives to change. He tolerated the boredom of his job because he worked beside his buddies, eager to share jokes on the job and drinks afterward. Yet too often, Duke had talked of quitting, until Trish felt like his mother, sending him off to school on test day. Duke had never wanted a greater challenge than collecting his paycheck.

Sam didn't even seem to care about that. True, he'd started off energetically this morning. With a shiver of pleasure, Trish relived the energy of Sam's kiss before pushing the memory from her mind. She needed to finish this quilt for her customer, not daydream about romance.

When the alarm sounded at eleven-thirty, Trish set aside her quilting and went upstairs to the kitchen. Tyler's school day ended at two o'clock. She'd have plenty of time to feed Sam and send him on his way before she returned home with Ty.

She couldn't let Sam leave without something to eat. She would insist, as an expression of her gratitude for his hard work. He probably wouldn't have anything to eat otherwise, unless he got it from Jenny. Trish prepared a salad and cold roast beef sandwiches, hoping that would fill him.

She entered the garage from the door off the kitchen. Sam cut off lengths of board with a power saw of some sort. Knowing he wouldn't hear her call or approach over the whine and not wanting to startle him, Trish leaned her shoulder against the doorframe and waited.

She watched the precision with which Sam cut the board, the assurance he showed using the saw. With skills like these, surely he could apprentice as a carpenter and earn his union card. If he wanted a job.

Smelling paint, Trish scouted the garage from where she stood. To the front of the garage, painted boards stood on newspaper.

The buzzing whine stopped, leaving the room unnaturally loud with silence.

"Hey," Trish called.

Sam spun toward her. "Hey, yourself."

"I have lunch ready when you get to a stopping point."

"That wasn't necessary." He grinned. "Don't get me wrong, I'm starving. I just meant I didn't expect it."

Trish swallowed, wondering how literal that "starving" remark might be. She tried a smile, feeling the pull of taut cheek muscles. "Well, from now on, you can expect it. I feed my hired hands."

"I appreciate it, ma'am." Sam pretended to touch the

brim of a non-existent hat. "I need to sand off the rough end here and throw on some paint. It'll take me about seven minutes."

Trish raised her brow, a smile coming more naturally to her face. "Seven?"

Sam laughed. "Can't do the job right in only five, and I'm too hungry to wait ten."

She nodded, feeling sick, and went back inside.

CHAPTER FIVE

Sam grinned and shook his head at Trish's retreating back, taking a moment to admire the feminine sway of her hips. He'd never figure her out. He'd have to work on getting her to lighten up some.

He sanded the rough ends of the board, stopping to slide his hand down its length. He enjoyed working with wood. Even more than that, he liked knowing Trish's porch would be safer for her and her son.

Sam reached for the paint can with a grimace. He'd hate to meet the unimaginative person who'd chosen these colors. Brown, brown and brown. It couldn't have been Trish, not with her natural warmth and artistic flair. Her house looked like a giant ball of mud. She must dread going into it each day. Sam liked brown as much as any man, but from his experience building houses, he knew that other shades would have better suited this small house.

Completing the painting quickly, Sam cleaned the paint–

dark brown, of course–off the brush and wiped his hands on a rag. He chuckled, remembering his surprise when he'd seen the plastic bag full of cloths marked, "RAGS $5."

Still smiling as he entered the kitchen, Sam crossed to the sink to wash up for lunch.

"What's so funny?" Trish asked over her shoulder as she set out glasses.

"You." Her raised eyebrow made Sam grin wider. "You own a fabric store, but you buy rags? Doesn't Tyler ever outgrow his clothes?"

Laughter sparkled in her green eyes like sunshine on emeralds. "I may own a fabric store and have an active, growing son, but I'm also a quilter. Any material I can't re-use is less than one inch square."

Sam laughed, picturing himself cleaning paint brushes with scraps that small. She gestured him over to the table where she had set out salads and roast beef sandwiches, the one on his plate twice the size of hers. His stomach growled as he inhaled the delicious aromas.

"I bought the rags from an organization for the disabled." She hunched her shoulders in a shrug. "I'm a pushover when kids come to the door."

Sam nodded, liking this soft side to her. "Lunch looks great. I really appreciate this." As he sat down, the toy horse sitting on the pass-through shelf caught his eye. "That horse still in trouble?"

Trish glanced over her shoulder, then turned back to him with a grimace. "After only five days, I'm ready to cave in."

"Tyler giving you a hard time?" Sam bit into his sandwich, savoring the delicious roast beef and the tang of horseradish.

"No, that's the worst part. He hasn't said a word. He just stares at Horsey so mournfully at meal times, I can barely swallow. I think he understands this is fair punishment." Trish shrugged. "Maybe he thinks if he squawks about it, I'll throw Horsey in the trash."

The food stuck in Sam's throat. He drank a little milk to help it down. He remembered his own mother's idea of justice. He hated to think that Trish resembled his mother in this, too, believing that punishment equaled discipline. To throw away a kid's favorite toy was nothing less than emotional abuse. Sam had first-hand experience with that kind of child-raising.

"Would you do that?" he asked quietly, unable to remain quiet. Someone had to defend poor Tyler. "Do you really think it would be fair to punish him that severely?"

Trish set her sandwich down, eyeing Sam as she finished chewing. He waited while she drank some milk. When she blotted her mouth with a green cloth napkin, he wanted to reach over and shake the answer out of her.

"No," she said.

Sam waited. She sat silent, her steady gaze holding his. He cursed himself for a fool. Of course she wasn't going to throw Horsey away or she would have done it immediately.

"My mother would have." He owed her an explanation for doubting her parenting methods. Here she was, raising the kid on her own, and he comes in from nowhere, childless himself but questioning her abilities. He wouldn't blame her for being angry.

Trish went to the refrigerator. Returning with the bottle of milk, she refilled his glass then her own.

Sam took that as an encouraging sign. At least she didn't kick him out. He was pleased when she sat back down after putting the milk away and continued eating, without a question about his mother. For some reason, that compelled him to confide in Trish.

"My mother is a successful financial consultant. I'm really proud of her. She worked hard in the corporation to get the recognition she deserves." Sam grimaced. "She just wasn't real good at the things that are important to little boys."

Trish leaned forward on her elbows. "And just what might some of those things be?"

Sam lifted one shoulder, uncomfortable with how much of himself his answer might reveal.

"I'd like to know, since I have a little boy."

He looked into her eyes and saw caring, not challenge. "I think Tyler's needs are being filled already, if they're anything like mine were." He shrugged again, hoping he was about to tell her something common to all children. He didn't want to sound like an idiot. "I just wanted a room mom."

"A what?"

"You know, the mom who went on field trips with the class and brought in cupcakes for birthdays and holidays."

Trish leaned back and smiled.

"The kind of mom who made costumes for Halloween and school plays. The mom who welcomed all your friends after school with smiles and cookies, and who didn't come in and tell you to behave yourselves." He grinned, encouraged. "The mom who didn't care if you got dirty because you were a kid and she had a washing machine and that's what play clothes were for, anyway."

"Oh, I've heard of her," Trish said. "Saint Mom."

Sam scowled as Trish laughed.

"Sam."

Her reasonable tone alerted him that a lecture would follow.

"Those moms are the envy of every kid," she continued, "and the bane of every other mother who doesn't have the time to devote to twenty-five cupcakes or the talent to make a costume. I didn't have a traditional mother, either, if those are your requirements."

"You didn't? But you're the perfect room mom now."

"Please." Trish held up a hand to stop him. "Don't make me into some kind of paragon. I can usually schedule my work around Tyler's school events, but most moms don't have that luxury. Even if they don't work outside the home, they may have other children to take care of. Those of us with more flexible hours are expected to plan and attend all these events, as well as provide the treats."

He squinted in concentration. She resembled his mother and most of the women he'd dated, who–although maybe not consumed by their work–had few interests outside their chosen fields. Did she resent having to take time from her career, flexible hours notwithstanding? He took a moment to find a tactful way of phrasing his questions.

Trish sighed and leaned her elbows on the table. "I know I'm lucky to get to do these things and be there for Tyler. But I also have more obligations thrust on me than the mother who can't get away from her paying job."

Sam didn't know what to say.

Trish sat back again. "Sorry. I didn't mean to get on my soap box."

"I always thought room moms did all that stuff because they liked kids."

"We do, but it can still get to be too much sometimes. Often a mom volunteers because no one else has and help is needed." Trish stabbed at the last of her salad. "Listen to me," she muttered, "Room Mom Advocate."

Sam shook his head, her comments whirling in his brain. "None of this applies to my mother. She didn't help out at all, except to send in a check. She sent the housekeeper to the bakery to buy cupcakes for my birthday."

Trish stared at him for a moment. "Don't you think your mom did the best she could? She saw to it that you got treats, didn't she?"

"Yeah."

"So, okay, she couldn't get the day off work for her son's birthday. Not many parents can. But she took care of it the best way her job would allow."

"Maybe," he muttered, unwilling to concede the point. His mother wouldn't have taken time off work if it had been offered to her. With pay. When the housekeeper brought in the store-bought cupcakes, he'd felt like a dog being thrown scraps under the table.

Trish cleared her throat. "Your parents must have been pretty well off to afford a housekeeper, especially one who doubled as a nanny."

"My mother worked hard to get ahead. She still does."

"What happened?"

Sam looked at Trish, who kept her gaze fixed on her plate. "What happened to what?"

"To you." She darted a glance at him, but averted her eyes too quickly for him to read them.

He frowned. "What do you mean? Nothing happened. Mother worked; I grew up. Ann, the housekeeper, had to quit when I was about eleven to take care of her husband, who'd had a heart attack. I convinced my mother I was too old for a baby-sitter, so she hired a woman to come in twice a week to clean."

Sam heard Trish growl under her breath. He couldn't understand why. He'd answered her questions.

"So, what about your dad?"

He smirked. "Dad made Mother look like Parent of the Year."

Trish winced. "Sorry I asked."

"He probably wasn't so bad." Sam shrugged. "My coming changed everything. He didn't know what to do with a baby, so he left."

"Oh, Sam." She laid her hand on his forearm. "That's awful. You both missed so much."

"I never knew him. Mother filed for desertion when I was eight. Half the kids at school came from divorced families, so I fit right in."

Trish squeezed his arm tighter.

Sam fixed his gaze on the toy horse. "I used to daydream about how great it would've been to have a dad, to have two parents who really cared for me. About what my dad was like and the things we would have done together. About my mom being home more." He glanced at her. "They say you can't miss what you've never had, but I sure did."

Trish came around the table and hugged him. He pulled her onto his lap.

"What did you want to do with your dad?" Her muffled voice came from the crook of his neck.

"I don't know. Everything. Nothing in particular. Just having him would have been enough."

He felt Trish's nod. She pulled back and looked at him. "I worry about that with Tyler. That he's missing something. I guess he is."

Sam swallowed the knot in his throat, tasting guilt. He hadn't thought of Trish's circumstances while complaining about his past. "He has you."

"I try to make it up to him for not having a father, but I know a mother isn't enough. Sometimes it's easier to deal with the most demanding customer or delivery mix-up than to face Tyler's need for a dad."

Holding Trish in his arms, hearing her words, Sam let go

of the last crumbs of resentment he'd held against his mother. She'd done the best she could, given her need for security in her job. Something shifted in his chest, making it easier to breathe. An old pain dislodged, an unanswered wish fled.

He took a deep breath and filled himself with the essence of Trish. Exerting the slightest pressure on her spine, he eased her closer, wanting to lose himself in the warmth of her kiss.

Her eyelids slid half-closed, giving her a slumberous, immensely desirable look. Her parted lips neared his.

The doorbell rang, jerking them apart. Trish jumped off his lap as if scalded, looking like she'd be heading to the confessional for this one embrace. She wiped her palms down her pant legs with a self-conscious laugh.

"I'd better see who's there." Trish hesitated in the doorway, then turned to face him. "But hold that thought." She gave him a saucy wink before leaving the room.

Sam blew out the breath he'd been holding. Her guilty expression had scared him for a minute.

"No, it's fine," he heard Trish insist from the living room. "I want you to meet him."

Sam rose to greet Trish's guest.

"Sam," she said, walking into the kitchen. "I'd like you to meet my in-laws, Miriam and Jock Howell. Miriam, Jock, this is Sam Carrow."

Her in-laws. Great. Sam held out his hand to the

sixtyish-looking man, whose faded blue eyes assessed him thoroughly. A little shorter than Sam, Jock stood about six feet tall. He held his broad shoulders straight, giving a further impression of strength and reliability. Judging by his tanned face under a tight cap of wavy, snow-white hair, Jock enjoyed the outdoors.

"Pleased to meet you," Sam said. If the man had been anyone other than Trish's former father-in-law, he would have meant it.

Catching Trish's expression as he turned to greet Miriam, Sam got another surprise. Trish was wringing her hands together and worrying her bottom lip between her teeth.

Sam groaned to himself. He'd like to soothe that lip with his kisses. He yanked his gaze away from Trish and nodded at Miriam. "Ma'am." After a moment, he let his hand drop before it became obvious he'd extended it. This woman did not shake hands. Especially not with a man she'd found in Trish's kitchen.

Her thin, colorless lips disappeared as she dipped her graying head in a barely civil acknowledgement. Bone thin, her powdery skin heavily lined, the woman appeared to be in her sixties also.

In disposition, the couple seemed poles apart. When Miriam turned toward Trish, a chill shook the air that frosted

Sam's skin.

"I'm sorry if our dropping in is inconvenient, dear." She nodded at the table. "We didn't know you were...entertaining."

Sam's mouth dropped at her insinuation, as though the table held evidence of an orgy rather than lunch. Jock studied the toes of his loafers, tipping his shoe up as if looking for scuff marks. Miriam stood rigid, staring at Trish and waiting for a response. Trish smiled–

Sam did a double take. Yes, Trish actually smiled at the old witch and shook her head as he imagined she would at Tyler's antics.

"Sam's not here to entertain me, Miriam. He's doing some repairs around the house."

"Wish I could help you with that," Jock said, "but I have to hire out work myself. Arthritis, you know. I leave the hard work to the young men."

"You ought to hire Sam for some of the jobs you need done."

Sam jerked his head so hard in her direction, he figured he'd need a chiropractor. What was she thinking? He couldn't work for anyone. His company had so many jobs awaiting decent weather, he and his crew would be run ragged as it was.

Not that Trish understood any of that, given he hadn't told her the truth about himself.

"Our Elliott was young," Miriam said. "Only twenty-eight."

Sam swung his attention toward her. "Elliott? I thought your son's name was Duke."

Miriam giggled, sounding less amused than a dying wren. Judging by the discordant noise, she didn't make a practice of gaiety.

"He was named after me. Elliott is my maiden name. His father–" Who was awarded a derisive look. "Nicknamed him Duke after John Wayne. The man's crazy about Westerns."

Jock laughed and raised his palms. "Guilty as charged. The little guy earned it, though. When he was somewhere around three, he had a hobbyhorse he had to be pried off of, and a cowboy hat he removed only at bedtime and bath time."

Trish glanced at the toy horse on the shelf. "Tyler's like that about some things."

"That was a long time ago," Jock said, "but I think Miriam's still holding it against me."

Miriam sucked in an indignant breath that puffed up her small chest. "I don't carry grudges, Jock Howell. Life's too short not to forgive people their shortcomings."

Sam contained a disbelieving snort. Obviously she still considered her husband's action as part of his "shortcomings." Jock laughed outright. Trish smiled only faintly. Sam wondered if she'd been "forgiven" a few times by Miriam.

"Life is short, Miriam. That's why I'm looking forward to retirement. I've seen too many friends work until they had to retire due to poor health, and then what kind of leisure years do you think they had?" He shook his head. "No, sir, I'm not waiting till I'm too sick to enjoy my time off. I have eight months to go, and then Miriam and I are off to golf heaven."

"I didn't know you'd taken up golf," Trish said. "I thought tennis was your game."

"It was, but Miriam convinced me I'm too old for a strenuous game like that. So, I'm learning golf, which you can play much later in life. I'm trying to get Miriam to take it up."

"Oh, you should, Miriam," Trish said, obviously ignoring the woman's pinched expression. "It would be great exercise for you both."

"The clothes are ridiculous."

Trish chuckled. "You can wear whatever you want."

An uncomfortable silence settled over the room. Sam searched for something to say. Jock seemed friendly enough. "What kind of work are you retiring from, Jock?"

Trish shot Sam a startled, even panicked look which he didn't understand.

"I was with the Coast Guard, but now I'm strictly on office duty."

"What do you do, Mr. Carrow?" Miriam asked.

Sam rocked back on his heels, understanding Trish's

expression too late. She didn't want him to admit to being "unemployed," and he didn't want her to know his true financial status. Trish appeared to be a nice woman, but he keenly remembered Jenny saying Trish planned to marry a rich man next time. Now that he'd started to get to know Trish, the knowledge throbbed like a splinter under his skin.

She caught his eye and gave him a tiny smile. "Right now, Sam's fixing the porch for me, as I told you earlier. And high time, too. I've been afraid that Ty would fall through."

"I totally agree, dear," Miriam said.

Three amazed faces turned her way. "You do?" Trish asked.

"This house is none too safe, now that Elliott isn't here to maintain it. That's why I keep saying you and Tyler should move in with us."

"Yikes," Trish exclaimed.

Miriam gasped. Jock choked on a cough that could have covered laughter or indignation. Sam watched a furious red burn across Trish's creamy skin. She held up her arm, indicating a wristwatch. "I meant, 'Yikes, look at the time.' I need to go get Ty now."

"But that's why we came," Miriam said. "We wanted to pick up little Tyler from school and take him to get his picture made with Santa Claus."

Sam stared in disbelief. Wasn't taking your kid to visit Santa a parent's job, one of the joys of the season? Okay, so his mother had delegated the chore to the housekeeper, but Sam hoped Trish would want to go with Tyler herself. He wanted to kick himself for hoping, but he couldn't seem to help it. Her controlled expression gave him no clue to her feelings.

"I'm sorry, Miriam," Trish said, "but I'm making Tyler a suit for Christmas, and it isn't done yet. I'm planning to take him Saturday. You're both welcome to come along then."

"Oh, no, dear. Saturdays at the mall are much too crowded for me. The lines are so long, it would take hours. If we take him right after school, we'll be done in time for supper."

"That's true, but–"

"Does Tyler still like that nasty-smelling Oriental food? I thought we'd take him out to eat before bringing him home. Make a real celebration of it. Then you wouldn't even have to cook, dear."

Not if Trish wants to skip dinner herself. Sam glowered. How thoughtful of the old hag. Although, from her comment on Oriental food, Sam imagined sitting through dinner with Miriam at a Chinese restaurant wouldn't exactly be a joy.

"That's very thoughtful, Miriam," Trish said, startling Sam as she repeated his thoughts. "But his suit still–"

"Oh, I have that problem solved, too." Miriam waved her

hand at Trish as though shooing a pesky fly. Her lips rose in what Sam guessed passed for her smile. It looked a lot like the grimace she'd worn since meeting him, only tighter and higher. "I've brought Elliott's suit for Tyler to wear."

Trish winced, although Sam doubted the other two noticed. Jock went back to studying the floor, and Miriam looked too darned pleased with herself. Sam waited for Trish to unlock her back teeth and give the woman the set-down she deserved for her meddling.

And he waited.

Trish's hands clenched and relaxed a few times, while a muscle ticked in her cheek. Finally, Sam understood she was battling with herself. He admired Trish's tolerance, but he wondered when she'd put Miriam in her place.

"Well?" Miriam prompted, her smile not faltering a millimeter, as she seemed very sure of herself.

"Well, I can foresee a few problems with that plan, Miriam."

"Oh?" Miriam arched a thin brow.

"Yes. This may be the last year Tyler believes in Santa Claus. He already has his doubts." Trish glanced Sam's way before returning her gaze to Miriam. "I'd like to be there myself."

"But then it wouldn't be special."

Trish arched her eyebrow right back at Miriam. "Oh?" she repeated in a voice just as cool as her former mother-in-law's had been.

"I didn't mean that the way it sounded, dear. I only meant it wouldn't be an outing with just his grandparents if you came."

"I understand what you meant," Trish said with a small smile.

Sam decided right then never to get her mad at him.

"Here's what I suggest," she continued. "Why don't we wait until tomorrow night? I'll finish Tyler's suit this evening, and we'll all go see Santa together."

"But–" Miriam interrupted.

"Wait." Trish held up her hand. "We can all watch Ty with the jolly fat man." She slid another glance over at Sam. "You two can take him to dinner. I'll stay at the mall and shop."

Miriam looked from Trish to Sam and back again. Sam wanted to reassure Miriam he wasn't part of the group going to watch Tyler with Santa.

"That sounds good." Jock's voice boomed unexpectedly into the silence. He grabbed his wife's elbow. "Can't ask for any more fair than that, Miriam."

"I suppose not. But there's no reason for you to go to all that trouble sewing, Trish, dear. We have Elliott's suit all ready. I even starched the collar on the little white shirt so it would stand up crisp and new-looking." Miriam pulled a tissue from her sleeve. She dabbed her eyes, then touched the tissue delicately to her nose. "I'm sorry. I shouldn't cry. It was just handling my son's clothes and knowing he'd never see his own son wear them." Miriam pressed the tissue against her mouth. Her shoulders shook, and a tiny whimper escaped.

Sam watched in wide-eyed disbelief, barely able to keep his mouth from hanging open in awe. If she weren't so melodramatic, he might have applauded. Jock patted her back, saying, "Here now" and "There, there." Sam turned to see Trish's reaction. Surely, she couldn't be buying into this, too?

Trish wore her no-expression look again. She had jammed her fists into her pants pockets, and her arms were locked straight. She rocked from heel to toe and back, biding her time. Sam couldn't help but wonder if she was battling herself again or searching for another compromise. He hoped for Tyler's sake she wouldn't give in. Just the mention of a starched collar made Sam's neck itch.

"I'm sorry," Miriam said after another moment. She sniffed, then raised her head to look at Trish through wet, mournful eyes.

Trish crossed the space that separated them and hugged her mother-in-law. Sam's chest ached, both for Tyler having to wear the old suit and stiff-collared shirt, and with his own disappointment. He couldn't believe she'd caved-in to emotional blackmail.

"There, there, now, Miriam." Trish pulled back, but left her hands cupped around the older woman's shoulders. Unable to see Trish's face, Sam leaned closer to hear every nuance. "I think your reaction has solved the problem of what Tyler should wear."

Jock shifted his weight, looking as though he'd like to leave the room.

"It has?" Miriam asked in a wavering voice.

"Certainly." Trish slid her right arm behind Miriam's back with an affectionate squeeze as she spun to face Sam. She hooked her left hand around Jock's upper arm. "Ty will just have to wear the suit I'm making him."

Miriam gasped.

"No, it's too upsetting for you to even see Duke's old clothes. Just think how distraught you'd be if Tyler actually wore them. I wouldn't do that to you." She smiled. "We can't have you weeping in front of Santa. And think how upset poor little Tyler would be, knowing he'd made his grandma cry."

Sam wanted to shout with laughter. He would definitely be careful if he ever had to cross swords with Trish. She could fight dirty if she had to. He admired the way she'd used Miriam's act against her.

"But I wouldn't cry."

Trish pulled Miriam to her in another hug. "You obviously can't help yourself. It's okay. We understand." She patted Miriam's arm. "Now, I really must go. Tyler gets out of school in half an hour, and I have a few stops to make on the way."

Trish released Miriam and deftly turned Jock toward the living room. Sam followed along behind a quiet Miriam, unwilling to miss the rest of the show. Trish embraced Jock, who wrapped her in a suffocating bear hug before walking out onto the porch.

Trish bent down to kiss Miriam's cheek. "I'll see you tomorrow."

Sam caught Miriam's reflection in the mirror as she stepped around Trish and headed for the door. Her lips had disappeared again, and her eyes burned like hot steel.

She looked so evil he was surprised he could see her reflection.

As the couple went down the porch steps, Trish paused in the open doorway and leaned back toward Sam. In a low voice, she said, "Come out on the porch with me and wave goodbye. That'll really tick her off."

CHAPTER SIX

Trish walked out onto the porch. She didn't regret the impulse to tweak Miriam's nose, especially when Sam stepped out next to her and waved at the powder blue sedan. Fighting the urge to link her arm through his, she couldn't risk peeking at Sam for fear she'd burst into laughter.

She enjoyed the silence for a moment, gazing out at the empty street. Checking under her shrubs by the driveway to see if she needed to rake, she did a quick double take. A two-door, white hatchback stood barely visible behind the evergreen hedge that half-blocked her view. "Is that your car?"

Sam stilled, then glanced at the driveway. "Yeah."

"The other day, you had a black truck."

He cleared his throat and shifted his weight. "I borrowed the truck from a place I've worked in the past to transport the shop vac from Bart's."

She leaned forward on her toes and looked beyond the shrubbery. "Nice car."

"It runs good for its age."

Trish raised an eyebrow at him. She'd kept up with changes in car models even after Duke died. The car was only two years old.

He shrugged and jammed his hand in his jeans pockets. "Burns oil, though. I should probably get a newer one."

But he can't afford it. Ashamed of her suspicions, she sought to ease his discomfort. "Why replace it if it runs?"

"Right." Sam turned to her with a grin lurking in his eyes and flirting over his lips. "That's some former mother-in-law you've got, if you don't mind my saying so."

Trish stared straight ahead. She tried not to chuckle, but her lips curved in a tiny smile. "She's a beaut." The she regarded Sam steadily until he understood how serious she was. "And I would mind you saying so, if you hadn't just been a witness to that little drama in the kitchen."

"Little drama?"

"Careful, Sam," Trish said softly. "She's family, even if Duke's gone."

"I stand forewarned." Sam rocked on his heels. "What if you get married again?"

"Miriam and Jock will always be family. They're Tyler's grandparents. Hopefully, my husband would be able to accept them, as well. Ty would be lucky to have three sets of grandparents, don't you think?"

Sam appeared to ponder that for a minute. Trish wondered if he was thinking about his own parents. But why would he? They were discussing extra grandparents for Ty if she remarried. She chided herself. He'd only kissed her, a wonderful kiss that had awakened her passion, but just a kiss, nevertheless. She planned to date him for the practice, nothing more.

"Tyler would be very lucky," Sam said. "Speaking of Ty, I'd better move on out of here so you can go get him."

"Don't worry about it." She led the way back into the house with a wink over her shoulder. "I don't really have any errands."

"Why, Ms. Howell, I'm appalled. You lied to that dear little old lady."

She laughed. "And I'd do it again in a second. Tact and patience go only so far."

He shook his head. "You excel at tact and patience. I don't know how you do it."

"Years of practice," she said with a wry smile.

"How long were you and Elliott married?"

Trish threw him a chastising glance as she led him inside, amused by his use of Duke's proper name. "Five years. And we dated all through high school, so I've been dealing with Miriam since I was fifteen. Half my life. But I was an old pro at dealing with manipulators before I ever met Duke."

"Oh?"

She gave him a knowing look. "You're not the only child who had difficult parents, you know. But then, Tyler will probably be saying that about me in a few years. All kids think their life is less wonderful than it's supposed to be."

"What was so less-than-wonderful about your life?"

Trish sank onto the worn couch and gestured for Sam to take the wing chair angled to the left. "Looking back, I know I had it pretty good. My mom's a gem." She smiled teasingly. "Even if she isn't a room mom type. She works as a Realtor, joyfully putting together the right family with the perfect house."

"But she didn't make a good home for you?"

"On the contrary. My mom is intensely *there* for us, my older sister, brother and me." Trish swallowed, missing her family, who weren't coming until Christmas Day. Three weeks had never seemed so long.

"And then there's your dad?" Sam guessed.

"Yes, then there's Dad." She sighed. "I love my father, but he was raised to believe the man is the master of the house, whose every whim should be cared for."

"Sounds good."

Trish closed her eyes. *I will not get involved with another man who expects me to be fulfilled by cleaning house.* "My mom insisting on a career offended his masculine pride."

"What does he do?"

"He's an inventor."

"That's an interesting career. What's he invent?"

Trish pulled at the threads on the arm of the couch. "Nothing useful. Mom supported the family, but we all pretended Dad did."

Caution darkened Sam's eyes. "What did his employer think of his inventions?"

Trish's smile turned down at the corners. "Sometimes he'd take a job, but then he'd get a brainstorm, quit, and go hibernate at his workbench. Meanwhile, he'd pull his famous emotional blackmail on my mom, demanding she cater to him so his mind could be free to create. When his inventions failed, he'd accuse her of causing it."

Sam muttered something that sounded like "selfish jerk."

Trish pushed her hair out of her eyes. "He complained that she was never home. My mother worked like a dog–in the house and out of it–to provide the only stability in our family life. She cooked dinner every night, even when she wouldn't be home to enjoy it."

"The ideal wife," he said.

"But that was never enough for my father. Like Miriam, he needs so much attention it drains you." She jumped up and retreated to the kitchen.

Sam followed. "Were any of his inventions successful?"

"He sold a few, which made life even harder in a way. If he'd always failed, he might have given up."

They cleared off the table together. The clinking of dishes filled the silence between them. After a few minutes, Sam said, "So, you got married fresh out of high school to escape your home life?"

Trish glanced over her shoulder as she rinsed the dishes. "No way. I was determined to have an education."

"Did you finish?"

"I have an MBA. I worked as a management consultant before Duke died, but owning the fabric store has always been my dream."

He leaned a hip against the counter next to her. His dark blue eyes probed for secrets. "Where did your husband fit into all this?"

She turned her attention back to the soapy water. "Duke promised me he was different from my dad." She strove to keep her voice even. "He said that I could depend on him, emotionally, financially, and every other way."

Sam moved to stand close behind her. "And could you?"

The heat of his body warmed her back. She longed to lean against him and absorb his strength. She longed to have his arms around her, holding her, supporting her.

But she had learned about leaning on people. For too long, she'd been denied support.

How could she tell Sam that Duke hadn't lived up to any of his promises, that he'd been as irresponsible as her father? How could she admit how gullible she'd been, accepting Duke's lies and his promises of tomorrow? How could she make him understand that she'd still loved Duke, even though the only promise he'd fulfilled had been starting a family?

She stepped sideways, grabbing a towel to dry her hands. "I really do have to go get Tyler now. Are you at a stopping point, or should I leave you to lock up when you're through?"

He snapped his jaw shut.

Even though the conversation had become too personal for her, Trish felt awful. She should have escaped more tactfully. He wasn't the hired help. He'd have taken a subtle hint to back off without her slamming the door in his face.

She hurried into the living room, aware of Sam following. His stare unnerved her as she found her purse and dug out her car keys.

He crossed his arms. "I take it you'd rather not talk about Duke with me?"

Trish flushed. "I'm sorry. I didn't mean to be rude. I guess it's just been an emotional day, what with one thing and another."

He advanced on her, holding her gaze. "And was our kissing one thing, or another?"

Trish cleared her throat. She opened her mouth, then closed it again without speaking.

"Uh-huh." Sam grasped her upper arms and pulled her nearer. His mouth closed over hers with thorough intensity. His tongue swept across her lips, clearing away any objections she might have made.

Not that she would have made even one. She was enchanted, adrift with sweet sensation. She cupped his cheek. Tiny stubble from his beard grazed her palm.

Shivering with delight, Trish placed her right hand on his chest. His heart raced beneath her fingertips, beating nearly as fast as hers. When he pulled away and met her gaze, his eyes flared with desire. She gulped down what little air she could draw in.

"I'll be back in a couple of days to finish the porch." Turning abruptly on his heel, he left.

*

Trish drove home from the school, for once not really listening to the adventures of Tyler's day at kindergarten. Sam's kiss had left her weak, yet exhilarated. She tried to think of something else, something that wouldn't make her tingle with excitement. She wondered when he'd be back. A couple of days now sounded like a long time.

So much had happened today. Knowing she'd have to deal with it later, Trish pushed the scene with Miriam out of her mind, but she couldn't forget the things Sam had revealed about his childhood. A workaholic mother who neglected her son. A father who deserted the family, waiting around till after Sam's birth, leaving him to believe he'd scared off his father. Two neglectful parents and a boy yearning for love.

Was that why Sam didn't have a home or a job now? Was he still looking for something that didn't exist, or was he cheating himself out of all the good things he thought he didn't deserve?

She hoped the housekeeper had had a loving heart. Trish shook her head, unable to imagine him growing up in a prosperous home. He lived a remarkably different life now. She couldn't understand his mother–a successful financial consultant, according to Sam–not helping him. Jenny had said they weren't close, but this surpassed ridiculous.

"Mom, are you listening?"

Trish glanced over at Tyler. Her heart filled with love. He would never wonder if his mother loved him. Although he didn't have a father, at least Duke hadn't run off, deserting the family.

"Mom?"

"Yes, tiger, I heard you. You finger-painted today, but

you can't show me what you did."

"No." The boy sighed with his whole body, terribly disappointed in his mother. Trish smiled to herself, having seen this act before. He wanted attention and store-bought cookies, but not necessarily in that order.

"We didn't *finger*paint. We *foot*-painted." Tyler giggled. "But I can't show it to you 'cause it's a surprise."

"Oh." Trish suppressed another grin. "Well, don't tell me about it, then."

"I can't," he said solemnly. "It's for Christmas. Mrs. Swanson said."

Trish smiled at the familiar phrase. His teacher's words possessed more power than superheroes.

"It tickled," Tyler said.

Trish blinked and glanced his way. "What did?"

"The paint between my toes. It was better than mud 'cause I could see the colors." He leaned over and confided, "We did red on one foot and green on the other."

Trish laughed. "But you're not going to tell me about it, right, tiger?"

He shook his head. "No, Mom. I can't. Mrs. Swanson said."

"Hey, Ty, guess what we're doing tomorrow night?"

His eyes lit. "What?"

"We're going with Grandma and Grandpa Howell to see Santa at the mall."

The gleam faded from his eyes. *Oh, no. Don't tell me he's given up on Santa.* "What's the matter, Ty?"

"Nothing." His chin firmed as he tightened his lips. Crossing his arms over his chest, Tyler turned to stare out the side window.

Trish knew if she waited, he would bring up whatever troubled him. She drove the last few blocks, then pulled into the grocery store parking lot. She opened her door.

"Mom?"

"Yes?" Trish let the car door resettle against the latch.

"Do I have to go?"

Her heart sank. He obviously knew the truth. "Of course not, Ty. I'm not going to make you visit Santa Claus if you don't want to."

His lower lip stuck out for a moment before he pulled it back in. "But I want to see Santa."

"You do?"

Ty nodded vigorously, his white-blond hair flying wildly around his head.

"Then I guess I don't understand the problem."

Trish watched his eyes fill with tears before he turned his head away from her. Her heart wrenched. This had to be serious.

"I just don't want to go with Grandma Howell." He turned his tortured expression her way. "Is that bad, Mom? Will Santa put me on the Bad Boy list now?"

Trish smiled and stroked a lock of hair back from his brow. "Santa won't think you're bad, Tyler, and neither do I. But why don't you want to go with Grandma?"

His lower lip disappeared between small white teeth. "She's going to make me wear Dad's smelly old suit."

Trish suppressed her smile. "Grandma does want you to do that, honey. How did you guess?"

"Because when I go visit, Grandma takes me up to Dad's room. Last time, we went in that big, dark closet you can walk into, and Grandma showed me all his clothes."

Trish clenched her teeth.

"I don't like that closet, Mom. And Grandma cries and looks at me funny. Sometimes she calls me by Dad's name. She holds his clothes up to me to see how they'll fit, and tells me where Dad wore them. But, Mom," he implored, "they stink. My eyes water, and I always sneeze."

Miriam's obsession with Duke's death had turned their house into a shrine. Taking Ty in the closet felt downright eerie.

"I don't want Santa to sneeze, too."

She laughed with relief at Tyler's simple view of the

world. Of course Miriam didn't mean to frighten Tyler. She was selfish and misguided, a lonely old woman with no son to mother. The most harmful result might be Santa overcome by the smell of mothballs. Trish followed Tyler's unspoken fear that Santa then might not bring him any toys.

Oh, for the innocence of youth.

"Trust me, Ty. That's not going to happen. Santa won't sneeze because you'll be wearing the suit I'm making for you."

"Really?"

"Really." She ruffled his hair with a caressing hand. "I've already talked to Grandma and Grandpa about it."

Tyler caught her hand in both of his. His shining eyes adored her. "Thanks, Mom."

Knowing such adoration was fleeting, Trish captured the moment in her heart. She'd need to remember times like this when Tyler grew older and more independent and nothing she said or did was right. When he was a teenager.

"You're entirely welcome, sweetie."

Later, she watched Tyler dunk his store-bought cookies in milk and pictured a young Sam eating with the housekeeper. That upbringing undoubtedly influenced him to this day. His story made her heart ache. She'd wanted to bundle him in her arms and hold him.

Trish bit her bottom lip. Maybe that's what Sam wanted, a mother figure. She didn't feel maternal toward Sam. She wanted to try dating, and he seemed like a safe choice. She'd never get involved with him, yet she found him attractive. If she could get the hang of dating again, she might start looking for a father for Tyler. He needed a male role model with good values.

Unfortunately, that left out Sam. Which was a shame, she thought with a sigh. He had potential, and he kissed like a dream.

She recalled him saying he'd missed what he'd never had. She, too, could dream about the life she could have had with him, how great it might have been, but know she'd never have it.

CHAPTER SEVEN

"Mom," Tyler called down the hall Saturday morning. "Nick and his dad are putting his new go-cart together today. Can I go over and help?"

Trish emerged from her bedroom, tucking her blouse into her jeans. Tyler stood with his hand over the mouthpiece of the telephone, stretching the phone cord to reach from the kitchen.

"Tyler, I've asked you not to yell in the house. And yes, you may go to Nick's."

"She said yes," he shouted gleefully into the phone. "Okay. Bye." After two failed jumps that made Trish wince, he hung the phone back on the wall. "Mr. McIntire's gotta buy some more screws, so he's gonna come get me."

"Finish your breakfast and brush your teeth."

"I know, Mom," he said in a put-upon tone worthy of a teenager.

Trish grinned at his back as he headed to the bathroom. She couldn't help sounding like her own mother sometimes.

Fifteen minutes later, she opened the door to Bart and Nick. The boy's dark hair lay every which way, thanks to the brisk breeze that came in with them.

"Brr." Bart rubbed his hands while Nick ran off to Ty's room. "It's colder out there than I expected."

Trish eyed Bart's tweed jacket with a smile. While it stretched across his broad shoulders, it didn't quite cover his stomach. "Bart, if you'd just admit it's winter, you could wear a sensible coat like everyone else. Denying the season is here won't delay the cold."

Bart shook his head as she'd expected. "It's not winter till the twentieth. I have two weeks to believe it's still autumn."

"You have two weeks to catch pneumonia. Jenny will scalp you if you're sick over Christmas."

"Don't say 'scalp.'" Bart's black eyes twinkled as he ran a hand over his balding head. Thin strands of black hair laced the top. "We big-brained men with extremely short hair are sensitive to words like that."

Trish grinned. "Oh, is that what it's called?"

Bart chuckled. His easy sense of humor was often at his own expense. "Big-brained short-hairs."

"Short-hairs? Is that like a terrier?"

Bart's laugh boomed across the room. "That's priceless. My poker group is looking for a name. I'll propose the Topless

Terriers next Friday night."

"Gee," Trish said with a straight face, "I thought Jenny and the other wives had a name for you already. The LDBG's."

Bart skewered her with a narrow-eyed glare. "Loud Drunken Bald Guys is not a nickname we brag about. I tried to get Sam to join us last night."

"Sam?" Trish's mouth went dry. Her heart hammered at the memory of their parting kiss.

"Yeah, you know, Sam. My best friend."

Trish recovered her composure, but her giggle came out high-pitched. "Doesn't he have too much h-a-i-r to play cards with you guys?"

"You noticed, huh?" His dark eyes turned speculative. "What do you think of him?"

"Bart, you surprise me. For a lawyer, you're about as subtle as a Mack truck. I expect this from Jenny, but you?"

"Okay." He held his hands up in surrender. "Just let me say this. Sam's closer to me than my own brother. If you guys get together, I think you'll make a great couple."

His earnest blessing touched her. Still, she didn't want to encourage any matchmaking. She smiled non-committally. "He's not my type."

Bart cocked his brow at her. "What's wrong with him? He's a nice guy, and he likes kids. Isn't that what women want?"

"He's too much like Duke. I don't want to go through that again."

"Look, I don't know much about your husband, so I can't say if Sam is like him or not. But don't judge Sam by the way Duke treated you." He shook his head and turned toward the hall. "I'll get the boys."

*

A few hours later, Trish read the note taped to Jenny's door. "Trish: Come on in with the ice. We're all in the back. J." Shifting the bag of ice and the bowl of potato salad in her arms, she pushed open the door and walked toward the kitchen.

"Mother," Sam said in his deep, familiar voice from the family room to her right. She heard the exasperation in his tone. "I understand you're working hard."

The rest of his words jumbled in Trish's mind as she froze in the kitchen doorway. She couldn't see him from where she stood, but his voice vibrated through her. Even though he lived with Jenny and Bart, she had expected him to be fixing up his house today. She'd discussed the need to keep Ty and the pretend Santa-to-be separated. Finding Sam here tilted her off balance like the fun house at the amusement park.

"If you could just come for a few days, Mother. Even the weekend after Christmas would–" Sam stopped speaking, presumably cut off. Trish had experienced the frustration of talking to a parent who didn't want to listen.

She set the bowl down on the kitchen table and eased the bag of ice to the floor with a quiet thud. She inched closer to the wall separating the kitchen and dining room, unwilling to interrupt his conversation. As soon as he saw her, she'd wave, put the ice and potato salad away, then go outside. And confront Jenny about his presence.

But just for a moment, Trish simply wanted to hear his voice and let its magic play over her while she relived their last parting. His exquisite, nerve-rocking, spine-melting kiss. Then she'd honor her vow not to get emotional about him. To just date. To protect Tyler. But this moment she took for herself.

From where she stood, she could just glimpse Sam's dark blond hair above a low-backed, hunter green chair in the family room, where he sat alone. As he stared straight ahead, she noted his strong jaw line and the classic outline of his profile. The words he spoke to his mother might have been in a foreign tongue for all the attention Trish paid to them. She luxuriated in his deep tone, like rich Scotch whisky sliding over her skin. Warm and smooth.

"Mother!"

Trish jerked.

"I'm sorry. I don't mean to yell, but you're not listening." He massaged the bridge of his nose between his thumb and forefinger.

"I told you to call me here," he continued. "I don't have a phone connected at my house, and I don't always hear my cell phone if I'm working. It's not at all inconvenient. When I'm there, I don't want to be disturbed by–"

Sam ran his hand through his hair, ruffling it. Trish clenched her fingers, wishing it were her hand stroking the silky strands.

"How can calling me here be inconvenient for you?" he asked in a disbelieving tone. "Oh, please, Mother. You've known Bart since we were kids, and Jenny's equally nice, which you'd find out if you came for the holidays. When's the last time you took off for Christmas?"

Trish sighed and tiptoed back into the kitchen. Sam was a sweetheart to want his mother here, but even Trish could tell the woman wouldn't come. She grabbed the ice bag and quietly pulled open the freezer door. Jenny had cleared a space, and Trish slid the bag inside. The door closed with a soft snick. She found a place for the potato salad in the refrigerator.

"There's no use calling me at work, Mother," Sam said.

Trish went still.

"Of course they told you I wouldn't be coming in. *I* told you that same thing. I'm not working there now. If you want to reach me, call me here at Bart and Jenny's." Sam growled under his breath.

Trish clenched her teeth. Why did his mother keep on about this? Couldn't she hear the hurt in Sam's voice?

"Please think about coming for– Yeah. Okay, bye." The cordless receiver settled firmly in its cradle.

She couldn't stand it. If she went in now, he would know she'd been listening. But how could she not go to him? She leaned around the corner and peeked at Sam. With his elbows planted on his knees, he had sunk his head into his hands. He didn't move.

Trish crossed the room and stood behind his chair. She gently placed her hands on his shoulders, feeling his start of surprise, but he didn't lift his head.

"It's me. Trish," she said quietly.

"I know."

He started to sit up, but she held him in place. With slow movements, she kneaded the tight muscles in his shoulders. He immediately relaxed into her care, moaning as her thumbs rubbed over a stiff spot. She continued easing away his tension for a few moments before her ministrations turned into caresses.

He grasped her hands, stilling one and placing the other palm against his cheek. He tipped his head back. "Hi."

"I didn't know you'd be here."

"I didn't know you were coming."

Their eyes met.

"Jenny," they said in unison. Trish joined in Sam's chuckle, remembering Jenny's invitation to lunch and her request for ice. "Are Jenny and Bart out with the kids?"

Sam's smile turned down at the corners as he shook his head. "Bart was called into the office, supposedly. Jenny asked me to help the boys. I wonder what emergency she cooked up for Bart to get me over here."

Trish sighed. "I wouldn't pardon Bart of matchmaking so readily, if I were you. He was singing your praises pretty highly this morning."

Sam's eyes twinkled. "He's bound by law to tell the truth, you know."

"Yeah, right."

His gaze locked onto hers. "What do you say we put our friends out of their misery?"

Her mouth went dry. "What do you mean?"

"Why don't we go out on a date?"

Trish straightened. She'd thought about going out with Sam for practice. Here was an opportunity to reintroduce herself to dating, if she had the nerve to take it.

He stood and came around the chair. "I should have phrased it better. That was juvenile. What I meant to–"

"When?"

"Say was that–" Sam jerked to a stop. "What?"

"Not 'what.'" Trish smiled, even though her stomach flipped like an Olympic gymnast. "When?"

"When? I don't know." Sam shrugged with a boyish grin that caught at her heart. "I didn't really expect you to say yes."

She laughed. "Then how about next Thursday? I can get a sitter for Ty. My assistant, Candy, is always willing to watch him."

"Sounds great." He shook his head and chuckled. "Well, actually, Thursday sounds like a long time from now, but I'm not complaining. What would you like to do?"

She took his hands in hers while she thought about it. His skin was rough, his palms smooth with old calluses. A working man's hands.

The irony struck her sharply. Trish dropped her gaze to the coarse, dark hair on the back of his hands. She brushed her thumbs across them, delighting in the tickle of the curling strands as they settled back in to place. She tried to think of something they could do for a small amount of money.

"It might sound boring," she said, "so tell me if you don't want to do it." She looked up into his eyes. "I'd like to drive through Miller Park and see the Christmas lights."

"I've heard that's supposed to take over an hour because it's so popular. Would you have time for dinner first?"

"Probably not." She squeezed his hands. "And I'd want to be home to put Tyler to bed. But it would be quiet. We could talk."

His eyes widened. He dropped her hands and stepped back. "Time to talk. Yeah, that's a definite advantage." He ran his hand through his hair. "Maybe you could let the sitter put him to bed, and we could take in a movie."

She crossed her arms over her chest. She didn't want to tell Sam this was her first date since Duke died. Initially, she'd been shocked and overcome with grief, then she'd been too busy getting the fabric store started, and Tyler took up a lot of her time. Putting Tyler to bed on a school night was important to both of them.

And why did Sam seem reluctant to talk to her?

"Okay." He held his hands up in the standard surrender pose. "I can see you're upset. I'll do whatever you want."

His willingness to please her made Trish reconsider. Ty wouldn't suffer from her absence one night. Maybe it would be a good introduction for him, to get him used to his mother dating. Candy could put him to bed with no trouble. Sam wasn't being unreasonable. Trish wracked her brain for a compromise. "I'd like to see a movie."

He brightened. "Really?"

"Yes. I always have to rent the things I want to see that Tyler can't. I watch them after he's in bed, while I'm sewing. The only time I make it into the theater is to see a family movie with Ty."

"Great. This will be a treat then."

She pointed at him. "Only if I get to choose it."

"As long as we see that new animated movie, *Conservation Mouse.*"

"*Conservation Mouse?*"

Sam nodded. "A mouse saves the beaches from planet-destroying litterbugs by becoming a pirate. He takes them all to a deserted island until they learn to respect the Earth."

Trish laughed, knowing there was no such film. She delighted in Sam's imagination and his ability to tell a joke with a straight face. She gave him a cheeky smile. "I saw it last week."

He chuckled. "Next time, I get to go with you and Tyler."

"It's a deal. But this time, I pick." She named a legal thriller playing at the local budget theater. As long as they steered clear of the concession stand, the evening wouldn't even cost Sam twenty dollars–providing he had twenty dollars. Trish wondered if he'd be offended if she offered to go Dutch.

"You're sure you're not disappointed about the park?" he asked.

"No." Although Miller Park would have been practically free, too. "Tyler and I can go see the lights some other night."

"I wish I could go with you. His face will light up

brighter than those displays. I've read they're spectacular."

She was tempted. Sam looked as crest-fallen as Ty would if denied a treat. Knowing she'd regret it, she asked, "Did you ever do that when you were little?"

"No. We didn't have organized displays like that in our town. Sometimes if we were out at night, Ann drove me past the decorated houses."

"Ann?"

"The housekeeper."

"Oh." She knew she shouldn't have asked. *The housekeeper.* Those two words echoed in Trish's head. She stopped fighting the inevitable. "Then come with us."

"What?"

"We'll go Tuesday night. If we start by seven o'clock, I can have Ty in bed by eight-thirty."

"Are you sure?"

"Absolutely." This felt right. Either Sam really wanted to go, or he'd caught her enthusiasm. "I'm absolutely, definitely, positively sure."

"No, really. Would it be okay?" He laughed. She swatted his arm playfully. "What about Tyler staying away from me because of our plans for me to be you-know-who?"

Trish considered it. "He's already been around you all morning. His room is mostly dark, except for his night-light.

He'll be sleeping on the 24th. I think it'll be fine."

"Great. We'll take my car. It's smaller."

She frowned. "Why would we want to take a smaller car?"

"Because, being the good mom you are, I know you'll let Ty sit by the window in the front so he can see better. In my car, you'll be pressed against me." Sam wiggled his eyebrows.

"The boy will be looking the other way. You'll be–"

"In the back seat."

He grimaced playfully. "Spoilsport."

After lunch, Trish sat with Jenny on the screened-in deck, sipping iced tea and watching the four "boys" assemble the go-cart. Heather snuggled on Jenny's lap, putting her baby doll to sleep and looking heavy-eyed herself.

"Bart was lucky to get his business settled by lunch time." Trish watched Jenny from the corner of her eye. "I thought he usually didn't have to work on Saturdays?"

Jenny studied her tea glass as a pink blush swept across her skin. She cleared her throat. "Yes, that was lucky, wasn't it?" She nodded out at the crew. "Sam's good with the boys, don't you think?"

Trish shook her head. "Jenny, you're as transparent as those storm windows. You sent Bart off to his office, got Sam here to work with the boys, and called me over with a plea for a bag of ice, all just to get me and Sam together."

"You'll get nothing from me but my name, rank, and cereal coupons." Jenny shifted her now-sleeping daughter in her lap. "I'm pointing out how much Tyler likes Sam and vice versa. See how Ty follows Sam's suggestions and makes sure he's always at Sam's side?"

"Jenny–"

"Don't 'Jenny' me. I'm going to put Heather down to nap. I'll be back in a few minutes."

Trish had had enough with the matchmaking. But as she watched the four heads bent over the go-cart, she noticed the things Jenny pointed out. Ty hung onto Sam's every word, eagerly doing whatever he said. She could hear the deep, compelling tone of Sam's voice. She, too, was under his spell, eager to please him, wanting to make him smile.

Her breath snagged in her throat when Sam leaned closer to help Ty turn a bolt with a big, open-ended wrench. They looked like father and son with their blond hair. Sam's large hand surrounded Tyler's as he steadied the boy's grip on the wrench. When Ty studied him, Sam tousled his hair. With his patient and gentle nature, Sam would make a wonderful father.

Would he even stick around to be a dad, or would he model his own father and run off in a few years? Did he realize the commitment it took to be a parent? Did he have it in him to stay through the bad times as well as the good? She couldn't risk Tyler coming to love Sam and then losing him. He'd already lost Duke.

Trish debated whether to stop her relationship with Sam. No dates, no practice. She'd be wiser to halt this now and go back to being friends, before she or Sam or, most importantly Ty, became too involved.

"Hey." Jenny's voice startled her as she came back onto the deck. "What, or should I say *who* are you thinking so hard about? Could it be Sam who's put that dewy-eyed look on your face?"

Jenny's teasing cleared out her worries. She'd agreed to a date, not a life-long commitment. "It could be. You can stop pushing me at Sam, by the way. We're going out next week."

Jenny's hoot of triumph caused four male heads to turn her way.

"What's wrong, Mom?" Nick yelled across the yard.

Trish laid her hand on Jenny's forearm. "I haven't told Ty yet," she said quietly, afraid Jenny would announce her date to the entire neighborhood.

Jenny patted her hand. "Nothing," she hollered out to Nick. "Just...something nice Mrs. Howell told me."

Sam grinned. Bart shot a look at Sam then grinned, as well. Trish tried not to squirm in her seat.

"How was your trip to the mall?" Jenny asked after a moment.

Trish made a face. "Not bad. Ty studied Santa so hard he could paint the poor guy's portrait. Then he asked if Santa had gotten his note yet."

Jenny winced. "Oh, no."

"Oh, yes. Fortunately, Santa ho-ho-ho'ed and said he gets all the letters. He said he hadn't read one from Ty yet, but he'd get to it before Christmas Eve."

"Bless you, Santa Claus," Jenny said.

"My thoughts exactly."

"And Miriam?"

Trish sighed. "She sniveled a lot about how nice Ty would have looked in Duke's suit, until Jock cut her off."

Jenny's mouth dropped open. "Jock?"

Trish nodded. "I was surprised, too, but he looked her straight in the eye and asked her if she didn't think Ty looked nice as he was. Instantly, Miriam became the doting grandma."

"Jock did that?"

"It's good to know he can. I don't know what happened during dinner, but when they brought Ty home, Miriam handed me Duke's suit and meekly asked–"

"Meekly? Miriam?"

"Miriam very meekly asked if Tyler might like to wear it sometime over the holidays."

"I can't believe it."

"Me neither, and I was there. Duke's suit is airing out in our garage. Ty can wear it to their house Christmas night."

"I bet she hits the roof when you tell her you have a date."

"Who said I was going to tell her?"

Jenny giggled. "Hey, I just remembered. Sam said something strange to me yesterday."

"What?"

"I'm to reassure you his furnace works fine."

Trish frowned. "Why would he ask you to tell me that?"

"Beats me, but he was pretty insistent about it." Jenny shrugged. "I'm to make sure you understood he wasn't going to lose his heat."

"That's good." She'd been worrying about him paying his heating bill.

"He doesn't have his thermostat set very high, though," Jenny said. "I was over there yesterday, taking him some lunch. The house was downright chilly."

"Good thing he's staying here then."

Trish worried about Sam for the rest of the day. After she tucked Tyler into bed, she dug through a trunk in her sewing room. Near the bottom, she located a half-finished quilt, which had been commissioned the previous summer by a starry-eyed girl for her trousseau. When she canceled the order, she told Trish to keep the quilt, not wanting any reminders of her unfaithful ex-fiancé.

Shaking out the material, Trish assessed the amount of work needed in order to complete it for Christmas. The top was ivory, the back forest green. The bride had requested a wedding ring pattern quilted in ivory-colored thread. She'd asked Trish to include two doves facing each other as a centerpiece in the classic layout.

Although Trish wasn't crazy about the design, she had to admit it made a handsome, reversible quilt. The top was an elegant ivory-on-ivory, and the dark green back showcased her delicate stitching. She only needed to bind it.

Calculating the time needed for a transformation, Trish figured she could start next weekend, as soon as she finished her custom orders. She'd appliqué some red berries and a bow onto each wedding ring, turning them into wreaths. The doves would have to resemble the peace of Christmas rather than a romantic pairing.

With a satisfied nod, Trish set Sam's present on top of the pile in the trunk and closed the lid. A wedding ring quilt might seem suggestive, but making the rings into wreaths toned it down. Even though Sam most likely wouldn't know the name of the pattern, giving him something to warm his bed felt intimate.

Trish turned out the light, thinking of other ways to help

Sam stay warm in bed.

Hormones, she rebuked herself with a wry smile, going to her lonely bedroom. *Go slowly. Proceed with caution. He's just practice for real dating later.*

Still, as she snuggled under her own quilt, she tingled with excitement. A date. With Sam. Holding hands and kissing goodnight. It had been so long, too long, since she'd felt this kind of thrill.

CHAPTER EIGHT

"Two adults, one child," Sam told the man in the ticket booth at the entrance to Miller Park. Tuesday night fell cold but clear, perfect for snuggling in his warm car and viewing the displays of Christmas lights.

"Only four dollars for a family," the old man said, clapping his hands against his arms. His wind-chapped face matched his red plaid jacket. He accepted the money from Sam. "You were right smart to bring the missus and your boy out tonight. Not as much traffic as on the weekend."

"That's what we hoped." Sam's voice sounded as hollow as his chest. He inched the car forward in line, wishing he had his own family to bring. If only Trish didn't care about snagging a guy with a fortune, he'd consider starting something with her. Ty would make any man proud.

He glanced at Trish seated beside him, and at Ty, over by the door where he could see better and share in the warmth near the heater. She stared out the windshield, not meeting his gaze. What did she think of the old guy calling them a family? Was she embarrassed?

"Look." Ty pointed ahead to the left, his gaze darting between them. "I see a big castle, like Santa's."

"I see it, too," Trish said.

Ty got up on his knees, then leaned across his mother. He looked at Sam with big eyes and an earnest expression. "Is it okay if I sit on my feet, Mr. Carrow? I won't tear your seat or anything."

"Sure, sport." Sam ruffled his hair. His arm brushed the front of Trish's coat.

She peered at him from the corner of her eye. Sam raised his eyebrows and tried to look innocent. By the quirk of her lips as she turned her attention back to Tyler, Sam knew she hadn't bought his act.

He grinned. What a great start to the evening. Having Ty along on their first date might work out well.

Suddenly, Sam's gut clenched in dread. What would happen when Trish found out about his construction company and his deceit? Would she pursue him because of his wealth or turn away because of his lies?

Clenching his jaw, Sam berated himself for a fool. What had he thought he'd prove by testing her? He didn't want either outcome. He just wanted a woman to put him first in her life. When Trish found out he'd withheld the truth, he'd be nowhere near first. He probably wouldn't be in her life, at all.

And if she wanted him for his money? Then he wouldn't want her.

"See that, Mr. Carrow?" Ty's high-pitched voice broke into his thoughts. "Those reindeers move. See? They're nodding their heads." He sat back and crossed his arms over his chest. "'Course, they're not real. They're only lights."

Up ahead, white lights wrapped around wire frames formed three of Santa's reindeer. Two nodded their heads, while another "nibbled" on the ground. One had a flashing red nose, which reflected on the snow. Sam inched the car closer. "They're still pretty cool."

Obviously, it was the right answer. Ty's eyes lit with excitement again, reassured he wasn't too grown up to enjoy the light show if Sam did.

Sam's chest ached. He wished this boy were his. He'd formed an attachment to Tyler right from the start.

Sam stole a glance at Trish, who had her head turned toward Ty, pointing out another animated scene. He wanted her, too, against his better judgment.

He couldn't understand why he'd set himself up again, falling for a mercenary woman. Then he recalled her loving manner with Tyler, her generous friendship with Jenny, her gentle care of Heather. Every aspect of her personality combined with her physical loveliness made her seem like the perfect woman.

His wealth was a reality in his life. If Trish could love him for himself not knowing he was wealthy, he could overlook her wanting a rich man.

Taking a deep breath for courage, he reached for Trish's hand, intending to just establish contact. She started with surprise when his palm slid against hers. Satisfied when she didn't pull away, he squeezed her hand, then loosened his grip.

Her fingers slid between his, holding his hand in place. He linked their hands together. Her brief, smiling glance warmed him from the inside out.

Sam released the breath he didn't realize he'd been holding. Maybe everything would be okay, after all. Maybe she'd understand about the lie, that he'd been cautious about starting a relationship. Maybe once she understood him better, she wouldn't take his reluctance personally.

He'd wait a little while longer to tell her, so she could get to know him. Maybe, if he was very lucky, she'd also fall a little bit in love with him. Then they would laugh together about his...misrepresenting himself. After all, she wanted a rich man. She shouldn't be upset to find out he was one.

Sam nodded, pleased with his new plan. He leaned toward Trish to whisper in her ear. The strawberry scent of her shampoo tickled his nose. "Is it okay if I offer to take you and

Tyler for ice cream after we finish here?"

Her gaze met his. "I'm sure he'd enjoy that. I appreciate you asking me first."

"Hey, I may not know much about kids, but I'm learning about moms."

For the rest of the ride through the park, their conversation consisted of comments on the light show. Sam enjoyed it almost as much as Tyler, since he'd never done anything like this before. He had the added bonus of having Trish pressed against his side and her hand clasped in his. His bright hopes for the future outshone any spectacle Miller Park offered.

*

"Aren't you excited?" Candy asked on Thursday evening.

Trish sat at the vanity table she'd received for her sixteen birthday. She raised a brow at Candy's reflection in the mirror. Candy had come over an hour early, presumably to watch Tyler while Trish prepared for her date with Sam. But so far, Candy had only hovered and given advice. Trish had changed clothes twice under Candy's critical eye. Now she wore a green sweatshirt with a snowman painted on it teamed with black denim jeans. She'd only seen Sam wear casual clothes and hoped this would be suitable. She sure wasn't changing again.

"Why should I be excited?" Trish suppressed a grin as she watched Candy's expression. "It's just a date."

"Just a date?" Candy dramatically threw her hands in the air. "Just a date, she says, like she has one every day. I happen to be your babysitter. I know how many dates you've had since Duke died."

"Okay, okay. But I'm really not excited."

Candy's shoulders slumped. "You're not?"

Trish toyed with the perfume bottles on her vanity so Candy couldn't see the doubts reflected in her eyes. Candy sank onto the bed behind her. "I'm scared," Trish said quietly.

"I thought you liked this guy?"

"I do. It's just... The last time I had a date, there weren't so many things to worry about."

"Like what?"

"Like me." She spun around to face Candy. "I knew how to date back then. I knew what to say. I knew the current dances."

"You're not going dancing."

Trish gave her a sour look. "I was a virgin. I didn't have to worry about diseases."

Candy gaped. "Are you planning to have sex with Sam tonight?"

"Of course not, but I'm nervous."

"Nervous is natural. Scared isn't."

"Until about an hour ago, I was so calm it was eerie. I felt as though I'd known Sam forever. Now I feel like I'm going out into the dark unknown with a total stranger."

Candy's face fell. "Because I upset you. I'm sorry."

"Sweetie, it wasn't you." Trish crossed the room and sat on the bed, enveloping as much of Candy as she could in a warm hug. "It's the idea of dating again at my age that has me so edgy."

"At your age?" Candy repeated. "You're only thirty."

"Right. Thirty years old and I've dated one man in my life, right before I married him."

"Sam's only your second guy?" Candy asked in amazement. "No wonder you're nervous."

Trish raised her brows.

"Not that you should be," Candy rushed on. "It's like a kid being left with a new sitter."

Trish peered at her, trying to follow her logic.

"You know, the kid cries for the first five minutes because everything's strange to him, then he forgets you're gone and has a good time."

Trish laughed. "I certainly hope I don't cry for the first five minutes of the date." She patted Candy's shoulder. "You're right, though. Everything will be fine. Now don't worry so much. It's bad for the baby."

Candy glared at her. "I won't attempt to comfort you if you don't stop teasing me."

Trish grinned. "Sorry."

"That's better. Try not to think of this as your first date with Sam. If you count Tuesday's trip to the park, this is your second date this week."

"Tuesday was different. We had Ty as a chaperone."

"If you're worried, I could go with you tonight." Candy's expression remained innocent and sincere even when Trish laughed. "No, really. It wouldn't inconvenience me, at all. I could even lean over the seat and give you tips whenever I thought you needed them."

Trish's anxiety disappeared at Candy's jest. "Thanks for the offer, but I'm going to pass."

"O-kay," Candy said in a teasing tone that meant "you'll be sorry." She crossed to the door, but paused before opening it. "Seriously, Trish, you'll be fine. You can handle this, just like you handle everything."

She seemed not to notice Trish's wince as she left.

"The great fixer," Trish muttered, sincerely and heartily tired of the role. She took a deep breath and left her bedroom, as ready as she'd ever be. Sam had arrived and stood in the living room, energizing the area around him. Candy sparkled with excitement. Tyler vied for his attention, jumping around him like a puppy.

Sam's easy laughter steadied her nerves. A royal blue, cable-knit sweater hugged his chest and shoulders. She waited for Sam to look up, curious as to how the color would enhance his already beautiful eyes. Jeans, faded a soft blue, clung to his thighs like butter on hot corn. Trish swallowed.

"I didn't hear the doorbell," she said, walking farther into the room.

They all turned toward her, but Trish concentrated her attention on Sam. His gaze met hers. The sweater turned his eyes a deep, midnight blue. She drew in a shaky breath. His eyes had darkened to that same shade during their passionate kiss the week before.

"Mom, can I go with you?" Without waiting for an answer, Tyler swung to face Sam and grabbed his hand with both of his. "You don't care, do you?" Ty turned back toward her. "Mr. Carrow likes me, Mom. He wants me to come."

Trish bit the inside of her cheek to keep from laughing. Ty, so precious and so precocious. "Tyler, we've talked about this. Mr. Carrow and I are going on a date. That's a different kind of outing than just going to see a movie. Remember?"

He frowned. "Yeah, but I still don't understand. I went with you guys last time."

Sam squatted down to Tyler's eye level and placed a hand on his shoulder. "It's like this, Ty. Sometimes two grown-ups like each other a lot and want to get to know each other better. So, they go out alone on a date."

Sam looked up at Trish and Candy. "Excuse me, ladies, I don't mean to be rude, but I have to talk to Tyler man-to-man." He whispered something in Tyler's ear.

Trish exchanged an amused glance with Candy, who not-so-discreetly flashed her a thumbs-up.

"But I kiss Mom all the time," Tyler said.

Candy giggled. Trish bit the inside of her lip. Sam's cheeks reddened, then he whispered something else to Tyler.

"All right!" Ty slapped a high-five onto Sam's hand. "See ya later, Mr. Carrow. Bye, Mom."

Trish grinned as Tyler dismissed her with a quick kiss on her cheek and ran off to his room.

"I guess we can go," Sam said. "It was nice to meet you, Candy."

Trish crossed her arms, not budging. "What did you promise him?"

Sam jammed his hands in his pockets. "I made a bird feeder for him from some extra wood I had. I told Ty he could help me paint it and hang it in your backyard. I'm sorry if I should have asked you first."

"I think that's sweet," Candy said quickly.

With a wry grin, Trish picked up her coat and followed Sam.

After Sam stepped out onto the porch, Candy called out, "Hey, do you have your cell phone? Is it charged?"

"Yes and yes. Why?"

Candy smiled. "It's a dating tradition. My mom used to give me a quarter for an emergency call, but a working pay phone is a rare beast these days."

"Thanks, but I won't need your help. I'm sure I can handle this."

Candy nodded at Trish's unspoken message of regained confidence. "I'm sure you can, too."

*

Trish drew a deep breath as she stepped onto the porch with Sam three hours later. "Thank you for a lovely evening. I had fun."

"I'm glad." He pulled her closer with his hands on her waist.

She slid her palms over his upper arms. He smiled and a shiver of anticipation trickled down her spine. She'd reacted the same on Tuesday, even with Tyler along. Every word and touch set off sparks then as they did tonight.

"I enjoyed the movie." She smiled as she recalled the intimate atmosphere of the dark theater and the thrill of just holding hands with Sam.

"Well, it wasn't *Conservation Mouse*, but it was okay."

She giggled. "That movie you invented couldn't have been as good. Everybody predicts this one is next year's Oscar winner."

"They only say that so you'll go see it. Besides, who said I invented *Conservation Mouse?*"

"I do." Trish gazed into Sam's eyes and heard the words echo in her mind. *I do.* The last time she'd said that to a man had been to Duke at the altar. She shook the image away, thinking how fast Sam would run if he knew her crazy thoughts. *Slow down.*

He leaned forward and brushed his lips across hers. "I love your smile."

She smiled wider, partly in invitation and partly because he affected her that way. Smiles just seemed to bubble up inside her whenever he was near.

He drew her into his arms and slanted his mouth over hers, warming her cool lips. She rose on tiptoe to deepen the kiss, sliding an arm around his neck to pull him closer.

"I hate coats," Sam muttered. Trish giggled in total agreement. He leaned his forehead against hers. "This should be where I ask to come in, but I won't. I know you need to check on Tyler. I just wanted you to know that I'd like to come in. I'd like to take this further."

She swallowed. "I'd like that, too."

Sam groaned. "Oh, man, I wish you hadn't said that. It's

hard enough to leave without you encouraging me to stay."

"Poor Sam."

"I'm touched by your sympathy."

Trish cupped his cheek. "Ty's spending Saturday night with his grandparents."

Sam stilled under her hand. His breath caught against her cheek. "What are you saying, exactly?"

"I'm not sure, exactly. I could make dinner here." In the soft light, she could see him searching her face. "I'm not offering anything else, Sam. I'm not ready for the commitment that comes with making love."

Trish groaned to herself. Had she really used the "c" word? Men hated to hear the word "commitment." His expression didn't broadcast his thoughts as clearly as she knew hers did, so she couldn't read his reaction.

"I'm not rushing you, honey." A ghost of a smile touched Sam's lips. He flattened his hand on her spine and brought her pelvis snug against his. "But I'm ready whenever you are."

"There's something we need to talk about first." She hesitated, searching for words. "Duke is the only man I've ever been with. We had a...a monogamous relationship."

Sam cupped her face, tilting her chin up until their gazes met. "This is awkward, isn't it? You need to know, but you're trying not to ask how easy I am."

Trish laughed. "For my sake, I hope you are, a little."

"Don't worry, sweetheart. All you have to do is smile. As to the other." He shrugged. "I've always taken precautions."

"Always?"

Sam cleared his throat. "Let me rephrase that. I used to move around a lot, going wherever the jobs were, which limited my chances to get to know a woman. I've outgrown casual sex, and I haven't been involved with a woman for a while. When I was with her, I used a condom."

The tension left her body as she sagged against him. "I'm glad we never have to discuss that again."

He brushed sweet kisses over her cheeks and eyelids. He nibbled his way to her ear. Delicious shivers skittered over her skin. "I'm looking forward to Saturday, no matter what happens–or doesn't happen."

She floated through the door, dazed. She hung up her coat and straightened her hair with unsteady fingers, too happy to keep a dreamy smile from her mouth.

"So," Candy asked from the kitchen doorway, "how'd it go?"

"Fine." Trish drifted into the kitchen and poured a mug of hot chocolate from the thermal carafe. After taking a sip, she closed her eyes and sighed. "Sheer heaven."

"The cocoa or the date?"

Trish opened her eyes. "Both."

"It's good to see you this way."

"It's good to feel this way."

"Did your plan to keep Sam away from the concession stand work?"

"No." Trish hid her smile behind her mug, recalling the brush of Sam's hand against hers in the popcorn tub. When they'd finished, Sam set the tub on the floor and reached for her hand. She hadn't held hands at the movies for six or seven years. She couldn't feel bad about the money he'd spent on the popcorn when it resulted in such simple happiness.

"Is Sam a good kisser?"

Trish smiled at her teasing and went into the front room, returning with the day's mail. Seated at the table, she set aside the bills for later and opened a Christmas card.

"Does it bother you that Sam doesn't have any money?"

"That's never bothered me," Trish said, slitting open another envelope. "I'm just concerned that he might take advantage of other people." *Like Duke and Dad.*

"But you're over that now?"

Trish put down the card and tucked her hair behind her ear. "Not completely. He seems sweet and genuine. But he has carpenter's skills he's not using. He likes kids, but he didn't get a holiday stint playing Santa. He could try for a job sweeping floors or emptying garbage for all I care, as long as he was trying."

"Mm. What does Jenny say?"

"I can't discuss this with Jenny. She wouldn't complain about Sam taking advantage of her, even if he was."

"Do you think he's tried and just can't find a job?"

She looked Candy square in the eye. "That's what I'd like to think. I'm too afraid of the answer to ask." After a moment, Trish cleared her throat. "How was Tyler?"

"Great." Candy grinned. "I think it did him good to see you go out and have fun without him."

"I get your not-so-subtle message."

Candy ducked her head back to her magazine.

Trish read her cards. She opened one with her in-laws' return address. A sweet, elderly woman in an apron graced the front, holding a platter of cookies. Trish rolled her eyes and read the greeting.

Her gasp caught Candy's attention. "What is it?"

Trish shook her head.

"You're greener than your sweatshirt. What's the matter?"

"It's a card from Miriam."

"Oh-oh. What's it say?"

"It's a lovely, innocent card. I'm sure I'm over-reacting."

Candy snorted in disbelief. "Innocent, from Miriam? You forget, I know the woman." She held out her hand. "Let me see it."

Trish shook her head and read aloud. "Dearest Trish, At this Holiest time of the year, I thank God for a daughter-in-law like you. I'm grateful you're such a good parent and role model for our little Tyler. It's shameful when a family is shattered by custody battles, like my friend Lucille's."

"Lucille?" Candy interrupted.

"Miriam's friend who won full custody of her granddaughter. I hear about what a great time Lucille has with Rose every time Miriam calls. She always sounds wistful."

"So this card is a veiled threat?"

"I have to wonder. There's more. She says, 'I'd hate that to happen in our family, dear. Fortunately, there isn't a need for it. We get along nicely, your family are dears, and there's no other family to interfere. Blessings to you during this Season and Always. Love, Jock and Miriam.'"

"Getting a compliment from her would sure make me nervous. She's the original smile-in-your-face, stab-you-in-the-back mother-in-law."

Trish clenched her hand into a fist, crushing the envelope. "If this is a threat, she'll be more than sorry. Nobody takes Tyler from me."

"It's so carefully worded, you can't take any offense. Why do you think she wrote it?"

Trish smiled ruefully. "She met Sam last week."

"Oh, dear."

"Exactly. He was fixing the porch, and I invited him to stay for lunch. Jock and Miriam dropped in."

"If she sends a sweetly nasty note like that over a casual lunch, what's she going to do when she discovers you had a date with him?"

CHAPTER NINE

Trish watched Ty run up the stairs at his grandparents' house to put away his things. Not in Duke's room, naturally. No one slept there.

After receiving that disturbing note, she hesitated to upset Miriam, but she had to straighten out this new problem. She wished Jock were home to run interference–not that he usually opposed Miriam, but it would be easier to reason with a reasonable person. Unfortunately, Jock was at his Saturday afternoon golf lesson, preparing for retirement.

"Tyler's been looking forward to his visit with you and Jock," she told her mother-in-law. "He's repacked his overnight case three times this week."

Miriam smiled. "We're glad to have him stay with us. It's lovely to have a little boy here again. My friend, Lucille, is so lucky. She gets to see her granddaughter every day, now that the girl lives with her."

"There's something I need to ask of you, Miriam." Trish

had to see this through, although she was none too reassured by Miriam's wistful tone. She took a deep breath. "I'd rather you didn't take Tyler into that closet full of Duke's clothes."

Miriam drew herself up to her full height of five feet and one inch. Her attempt to look down her nose lost its impact when she had to tip her head up to see Trish. Tightened lips accompanied a sniff of disdain. "It doesn't hurt anything."

"It upsets Ty."

Miriam pulled on a coat of indignation. "Nonsense. I would never do anything to upset Tyler."

"Not intentionally, of course, which is why I'm telling you this. That closet scares him."

"Tyler has never been frightened when he's with me."

"He wouldn't let you know because he doesn't want to displease you, but he told me. I don't want him going in there. I'm sure you don't want him too frightened to stay overnight."

Miriam cold, gray glare bore into Trish. "Is that a threat?"

"Of course not. I only meant–"

"Because I have rights, too, you know, as his grandmother. Rights any court in this state will uphold."

Trish swallowed her fear and anger. She strove to keep both emotions from her voice. "You don't have to worry about your rights, Miriam. I don't intend to keep Ty from visiting you and Jock. But I also have no intention of him being scared."

After a moment, Miriam's steel-lined spine bent slightly. "We don't do anything scary. I just show Tyler his father's clothes. I'm saving them for Tyler." She pursed her lips. "You never used to talk to me this way, Trish. I think that handyman you hired is a bad influence on you. I know he didn't like me."

Trish couldn't ignore the reference to Sam, but she needed to stay focused on Tyler. Miriam practiced manipulation as an art form. Sidetracking the conversation and turning the blame onto the other person were the tactics of a master. She'd learned that much at her father's knee. She inhaled a deep breath and blew it out slowly. "Sam doesn't have any influence, Miriam. My only concern here is Tyler."

"I'm concerned about Tyler, too. I can only imagine what he's learning from that man."

"And that's all it would be, your imagination. Sam isn't the issue here."

Miriam's moue of disdain looked skeptical. "Well, as soon as you hired him, you began thinking I'm trying to terrify my own grandson. I can't believe that's a coincidence."

Trish clenched her teeth. Losing control of her temper wouldn't further her cause. "I understand your good intentions regarding the clothes, but put yourself in Tyler's place. He's in a small, dimly-lit room. The air smells heavily of mothballs.

He's surrounded by his dead father's clothes." Miriam stiffened, but Trish forced herself to finish. "He doesn't remember his father, but his grandma, who he loves dearly, tries to make him be just like him."

"That's ridiculous. I love Tyler. I refuse to stand here and be talked to this way." She turned on her heel.

Trish quick-stepped after her. "Miriam, I'm not trying to hurt your feelings. I know you want Tyler to get to know Duke, but making him wear old clothes isn't the way."

Miriam whirled on her with clenched fists. "I suppose you have a better suggestion?"

"Show Tyler all those photos you have. Start with the picture on your dresser of Duke holding Ty as a newborn."

Miriam's pinched face relaxed a tiny bit.

"Get out your photo albums," Trish continued, hoping her words would make an impression. "Show him pictures of you and Jock getting married and having Duke. Let him see Duke growing up, and then having a son. That would make Duke more real to Ty than old clothes."

The reminder of the closet frosted Miriam's eyes once again. "I'll think about it." Miriam stalked down the hallway, her back as rigid as a flag pole.

Trish kissed Ty and let herself out. The confrontation had no doubt fueled Miriam's insecurity. Trish shuddered as she started her car. She couldn't think about a legal battle over visitation rights, or worse, custody. Tyler would be devastated by such ugliness. She doubted that she'd lose him, but the courts could be unpredictable, and grandparents received more consideration these days.

Her teeth chattered and she turned up the heater, although the car couldn't produce enough heat to warm her today. She drove home with extra caution, recognizing she was distracted enough to cause a collision.

Eyeing the snow-covered Christmas decorations lining the streets made Trish bitter. She usually loved Christmas, but right now, she lacked any spirit of goodwill. She needed to reorient herself. Sewing would soothe her. She would go home and work on Sam's quilt.

Sam. Trish drooped like a frost-burnt flower. She'd been as excited about their dinner tonight as a schoolgirl before her first date.

Trish drew herself up sharply. She wouldn't let Miriam's manipulations spoil her evening. With a quick maneuver, she spun the car into the parking lot of the grocery store.

She resolved to regain a more positive outlook. Miriam might threaten, but she wouldn't go through with a court case. She didn't have any grounds, for one thing. She basically wanted more attention and the reassurance she was loved.

Trish had made her point earlier, even if the conversation

had gotten nasty. Miriam wouldn't take Tyler into the closet today. Trish would treasure that victory for now.

Miriam would overcome her seasonal depression shortly after the holidays, as usual. All would return to normal.

It was, after all, the season for hope.

*

Sam rang Trish's doorbell later that night, then stepped back to test the boards he'd replaced. Strong and solid. He strode over them again, smiling his satisfaction.

"Admiring your handiwork?"

He swung around. "You caught me."

He stared at Trish, enchanted. She'd propped a shoulder against the doorjamb and crossed her arms over a butter-smooth, baby blue sweater. A navy blue skirt encased her slim hips. He couldn't believe he'd ever thought she looked like an angel. This woman was a walking temptation.

She swung open the screen door. "Come on in."

Her voice, low and husky, made his mouth go dry. He caught her in a gentle embrace. "Hi."

Trish's smile came slowly, then spread across her lips until it gleamed in her eyes. She slid her hands up behind his neck. "Hi."

Sam lowered his head to kiss her. He nibbled and lingered, satisfied just to be with her, not needing a cyclone of passion to sweep him away. This was enough. For now. The sweetness of maple met his tongue as he tasted her. He pulled back with a grin. "Are we having pancakes for dinner?"

"What?" She blinked in confusion.

"Your kisses taste like maple syrup."

"Oh." She smiled and stepped away from him, smoothing down her clothes. "No, I made maple bananas for dessert. It's not very fancy, but I got a little distracted while I was baking earlier. My amaretto cheesecake was a flaming disaster, literally."

Alarmed, he lifted her hands, inspecting them for burns. "Are you okay?"

Trish laughed. "I'm fine. The house doesn't even smell like smoke anymore, but I think I singed a few squirrels when I threw the cheesecake pan in the backyard. They've probably been poisoned on the charred parts."

"I hope you're exaggerating." Sam smiled, but images of her handling a fire alone settled like a stone in his gut.

She turned her hands in his, giving a brief squeeze. "Don't worry. I'm usually a better cook than that. I promise not to poison you."

"What distracted you?"

Trish's face clouded over. Her green eyes grew troubled and sad. "It's just Miriam again. I'd rather not talk about it."

Sam wouldn't coax her into a distressing discussion right

before dinner. As this was only their second date, she might not feel close enough to him to discuss her in-laws.

"I have margaritas, beer, and water. We're having Mexican. I hope that's okay."

Trish led him to the living room. As they sat on the couch and sipped margaritas, he could sense her unwinding. Her shoulders relaxed as she curved herself into the cushions. He pulled her over to snuggle against him. She nuzzled her cheek against his upper arm, and he reveled in her ease with him.

"What did you do today?" he wondered aloud.

She slanted a smiling gaze up at him. "Besides putting out fires and butting heads with my mother-in-law? I worked on a quilt for most of the day."

"I thought you'd finished your commissions."

"I have. This is a Christmas present." Her lashes dropped over her eyes.

Sam sipped his drink, relieved when she didn't ask about his day. He'd had to run to the construction office to decipher a plan with his foreman, then stayed to do some paperwork on the computer. Not being able to tell her the truth about something as innocent as office work bit at his conscience. She probably didn't ask about his day because she thought he'd loafed it away, being supposedly unemployed. That ate at his pride, but since he'd put himself in this position, he couldn't justify his annoyance.

"I found something interesting while I was straightening Tyler's room."

"Porn?"

She swatted his arm, laughing. "Ty's only five. I don't expect to find a dirty magazine for nine or ten years, if ever."

"You'd better change your expectations, then."

"Okay, Mr. Voice of Experience, how old were you when your mom located your hidden cache?"

"Eleven." He nodded as Trish's eyes widened. "And I was a late bloomer in my class."

"What did your mom do?"

Sam looked into his glass, avoiding her eyes. "She got a little hysterical, being a single parent and all."

"Hey, I resent that crack. Not all single parents get hysterical in a crisis."

"Sorry. I meant it was hard for her to be confronted with her son's budding sexuality."

She nodded and stood. "I can understand that. While I'm dishing up the enchiladas, you can tell me what your mother did when she found your dirty magazines."

Unpleasant memories hit him in the gut. "Trust me, it's not a pretty story. You'd dilute the salsa with your tears." He followed her into the kitchen. "Would you like to tell me about

Miriam now and get it over with?"

Trish grimaced, displaying the shy dimple that appeared so rarely. "Trust me, that's not a pretty story, either."

She busied herself with the side dishes for a minute. They sat at the table, steaming chicken enchiladas scenting the air. The first bite had him closing his eyes in ecstasy.

"Go ahead," Trish said, "I'm ready."

"Why, Ms. Howell." Sam clutched a hand to his chest. "You're so...brazen."

"Idiot." Her eyes danced with merriment. "'Fess up, Carrow."

He sighed dramatically. "Okay, you asked for it. I have no idea why Mother was even in my room. She certainly wasn't cleaning it."

"Because you had Ann, the housekeeper." Trish shot him a glance. "You're stalling."

He decided to tell it fast and just get it over with. "I had one crummy magazine. Unsure how to handle it, she sent me to have a conference with our minister." Trish's gasp made him chuckle. "The poor old guy didn't know what to do with me. I was already sorrier than he could ever make me. Mostly, we talked about my mother."

Sam chewed for a moment, collecting his thoughts. "After I saw her as a person, not just my mother, I was able to accept her flaws. I learned not all our problems were my fault."

Trish's eyes grew round. "That must have been some conference."

"I didn't get it all at once, but as the years passed, I understood better." He brushed her cheek with his thumb. "I talked with Reverend McCabe twice a week for two months. We covered just about every worry I had."

"Thank heaven for the Reverend."

"Amen." Sam cupped her face and kissed her gently, grateful for her entrance into his life. "He even explained that my mother needed her work to feel whole. 'Finding yourself' is a pretty hard concept for an eleven-year-old."

Sam searched her eyes for a reflection of her understanding. He wanted her to hear his meaning. "I've found myself just recently, and I didn't even know I was lost."

Their gazes met and held. Tension built.

Trish broke eye contact first, glancing down at her plate.

"So," he said to break the mood, "what did you find in Tyler's room?"

Trish bit her lip. "Another letter to Santa Claus."

He stared at her for a moment, struck dumb with the contrast of his guess of porn. He worked to suppress a smile, doubting if Trish would understand. Then he saw her lips quiver with the same effort, and he burst out laughing.

"What's his letter to Santa say?" Sam asked when they

calmed.

"You need to see it. It requires a response."

"Okay, remind me after we finish here. This enchilada is too good to let grow cold."

Over dinner, they talked about the Christmas program at Tyler's school, and his role as the innkeeper in his Sunday school play at church. Sam waited for her conversation to center on her business. When it did, he gave an inward sigh. Of course, her store came up in normal discussion, as would his business if he were being honest with her about his life.

Based on his experiences with Sherry and other ambitious women he'd dated, he expected Trish to expound on her problems at length. She outlined some issues at the fabric shop, but she didn't dwell on them. Sam waited, knowing more would come.

"Remember my telling you about Candy, my assistant? She started out as a short-term babysitter for Tyler, but has become indispensable. She's twenty-two now and expecting a baby. I'm trying to think of the perfect gift for her."

Sam blinked. She'd skimmed over her business problems and a small triumph of helping a difficult customer. Then she'd started talking about her friend. It confused him. Would she return to the topic of work? Now she was saying something about Bart and Jenny's party.

Listening to her, hope swelled in Sam's chest. She didn't

seem obsessed about her business. Maybe she wasn't a clone of his mother or Sherry or the other women he'd known. Maybe he could have a future with her, after all. His heart thrummed in his chest at the possibilities. Although her business was important to her, Trish cared for the people in her life.

Now, he just had to convince her he was one of those people. His heartbeat quickened. Being in Trish's life sounded good. At thirty-three, he was more than ready to settle down.

He helped Trish clean the table and rinse the dishes. He cleared his throat. "The other night, you asked about the women I've dated."

She turned to him, her mouth agape. "I did not."

"We discussed our past romances and physical closeness."

"Oh." She ducked her head, but he'd seen the blush flare across her cheeks. She put a bowl in the dishwasher. "That."

"I have something to tell you. It's about my fiancée."

She whirled back. "Your what?"

"My ex-fiancée," he amended quickly. "I've told you how dedicated my mother is to her work. It seems every woman I dated was working just as hard to get ahead in a career."

Trish frowned. "And that's bad?"

"No, of course not, in general. But not if it means losing

touch with what's important."

Trish's eyebrows rose. "You?"

"A woman doesn't have to take a back seat to her husband's ego. I'm not like your father."

Her start of surprise affirmed his suspicion Trish had been comparing him to the other men in her past, to her father and husband, just as he'd been comparing her to his mother and Sherry. It was only natural. But he wanted her to picture him in her life now. Somehow she'd become important to his future.

"It seemed the older I got, the more women cared about money, what my job was, my future prospects. I got labeled and admired for what I did and what I had rather than who I am."

"Is that why–?"

"Let me finish. This is hard enough as it is." He leaned against the counter, searching for words to complete his confession. "For some reason, most of the women I dated wanted to be seen with successful men. They enjoyed the elite venues money gave them access to. Being seen with a successful man, a mover and shaker in their fields, helped their careers."

Trish nodded. "And you resented that."

"Of course I resent that. When someone goes out with me, I like to know she's going even though she doesn't get her picture on the society page. I want to think she'd go somewhere no one would even notice her, just to be with me."

"Like to see *Conservation Mouse?*"

Sam laughed, partly in relief. She understood. "Yes, just like that. Not that any of them would have gone."

"And your fiancée?"

"She wasn't technically my fiancée since she didn't accept my proposal. Planning a wedding would have diverted her concentration from a project she had to see through at work, and the next project she wanted. She also worried that her boss would question her commitment to her job if she had a husband."

Trish's eyes widened. "You choose the wrong women."

"I know, it's partly my fault. Okay, mostly," he amended when she raised her brows. He couldn't believe his luck. He'd told her the truth about himself, and not only had she understood, she didn't seem angry. He winked. "I'm making better choices these days."

Trish laughed.

They settled on the couch with coffee, leaving dessert for later. "What happened today between you and Miriam?"

Trish sighed. "I asked her not to take Ty into their walk-in closet where Duke's clothes are stored."

"They still have his clothes?"

"Yep, from newborn to wedding suit. They're packed in

mothballs in his closet."

He shuddered. "Mothballs. I can understand why you wouldn't want Ty in there. Maybe I could get them some cedar boards."

"It's not just the smell. Miriam holds Duke's clothes up to Tyler and tells him where Duke wore them and what he did. It's her way of keeping Duke alive. Ty ends up thinking she's disappointed that he's there instead of his father."

Sam frowned, horrible scenes crossing his mind. He hesitated to voice such thoughts, but his concern for Tyler overrode his caution. "Do you think she'd mistake Tyler for Elliott? I only met her briefly, but she seemed pretty obsessed with her son."

Trish blew out a breath. "That was my first thought when Ty told me, especially when he said it scared him to go in there. Miriam is manipulative and insecure, but her mind is sound. If I had the least doubt, he wouldn't be over there without me."

"Of course not." Sam put his arm around her shoulders and pulled her close. "I take it Miriam was less than understanding about your concerns."

Trish's laugh rang hollow. "That's putting it mildly. She got offended and self-righteous. She accused me of being deliberately cruel to her." Trish bit her lip and looked down at her lap, where her fingers twisted themselves into pretzels. "It just got ugly. I'm hoping when she calmed down, she understood my intention to protect Tyler."

Her hesitation set off alarm bells in Sam's mind. What didn't she want to tell him? What else had Miriam said to put that shadow in Trish's eyes? "How ugly?"

"It's not something I want to discuss."

Sam didn't need the details. She'd trusted him with her emotions, a prized gift.

He stroked her hair, sitting quietly. Hopefully, sharing her troubles with him helped. He was getting more deeply involved, and while common sense warned him to back away from someone with this many problems, he wanted to take the risk.

Starting now. "You needed me to look at Tyler's latest letter to Santa?"

She rose. "It requires a response."

Sam followed her into the kitchen and sat at the table. She set the letter in front of him and leaned over the back of his chair.

Tyler worried that bad weather would keep him indoors over Christmas break, leaving him unable to ride his bike. He wanted Santa to bring it a week early. Sam grinned. "That boy's a rascal."

"Tell me about it."

"Do you want me to write him a note?"

"Yes. One of my customers works for a delivery service. She'll come next Friday after school in an elf costume with Santa's reply."

"That should convince a five-year-old. Can I be here when she comes?"

"Why would you want to do that?"

Sam leered. "Those elf costumes show a lot of leg."

Trish laughed and tweaked his hair. She brought him a green pen and red-lined stationery.

He whistled. "You think ahead."

"We aim to please."

Sam finished and underlined his initials with a flourish.

The note simply read:

> Dear Ty, I'm sorry to disappoint you, but I can't come a week early.
> It wouldn't be fair to the other children on my list. Christmas is the day we celebrate the birth of Baby Jesus. I think we should exchange presents on that day only, to keep it special. But I'll see you on Christmas Eve, as planned.
> Be good, S.C.

S.C., Trish noted. For Santa Claus or Sam Carrow?

"What do you think?" Sam asked.

I think I'm losing my heart to Santa. Sam had snuck past her defenses even before their dates. His concern for Tyler had tipped the scales in his favor. At that moment, having Sam in her life made sense. Single, relatively young, and definitely ready for romance, she wanted to pursue the possibilities of a genuine relationship. Not just practice for some other man, but a future with Sam. "It's perfect."

She waved him back from the table and, after he scooted away, slid onto his lap. Clasping her hands behind his neck, she whispered, "Should I tell Santa what I want for Christmas?"

Sam chuckled. "Have you been a good little girl?"

Her naughty smile made him catch his breath.

"Up until now."

Sam's eyes widened, and his arm locked her tightly against his chest. His tongue met hers, stroking, thrusting, imitating the act yet to come.

Trish shifted on his lap, then heard his frustrated moan. She broke the kiss and feasted herself on the sight of his strong, passion-flushed face. She trailed her fingertips across his cheeks, teasing them quickly across his lips before raking them into his hair. Pressing her forehead to his, she met his gaze directly. "The table's digging into my back. Would you like to go to my bedroom?"

"I thought you'd never ask."

CHAPTER TEN

Trish put her arm around him. Entwined like lovebirds, they walked to her bedroom. She pushed the comforter down on her bed, suddenly overcome with uncertainty. She hadn't had a "first time" in twelve years. What would Sam expect? "Do you want me to undress?"

Sam pulled her into his arms and took possession of her mouth. He ran his hands over her back, pressing her against him.

She circled her arms behind his neck, straining on tiptoe to deepen the kiss, needing to get closer. Her rapid breathing matched his. Her pulse pounded in her ears, keeping pace with his thudding heartbeat.

His hands slipped under her sweater, caressing her back, her ribs, sliding up over her shoulders. She leaned backward and drew the sweater over her head, thrilling as Sam's arousal thrust against her.

He kissed his way down her neck, tracing his fingers

over her breasts. Trish gasped, feeling the heavy throbbing low in her body. He kissed the tops of her breasts, blazing a wet fire downward. Her bra came unfastened. His fingertips smoothed it off her shoulders, leaving a wake of gooseflesh.

Sam glided his hands down and molded her bottom. She pressed nearer, wanting to lock her leg around his and bind him against her. Aroused as never before, she clutched his shoulder with one hand and drew his head to her breast with the other. Supporting her lower back, he tilted her, playing his lips and tongue and teeth over her pouting nipple. His hot breath warmed her. His tongue teased and tormented and made her hotter.

Sam unbuttoned and unzipped, and her skirt fell to the floor. Trish shivered, reveling in the power of her desire. She was damp and ready for him–and still half-dressed.

"Trish, honey, you're so beautiful." Sam devoured her mouth.

With one hand, Trish worked his shirt buttons open, not with speed or grace, but with overriding need. She pushed his shirt away, leaving him to discard it while her hands roamed.

He was all warm skin and firm muscles. She nuzzled her cheek against his chest. The crisp hairs tickled her, sending shivers of delight across her skin. He smelled of warm, aroused male. She brushed her tongue across his flat nipples, flicking them into small marbles. Trish licked her lips, trying to capture his faintly salty flavor.

His groan inflamed her, giving her the encouragement she needed to take what she wanted. A heady feeling of power surged through her as his body thrust against hers. She trailed kisses across his chest. Easing her hands down, she learned the texture of his hair-roughened stomach and firm muscles.

Trish stepped back and studied him, knowing he was also looking at her. As she undid his belt buckle, she met Sam's gaze. The passion in his midnight blue eyes set her insides throbbing. The empty ache between her legs begged for his body to fill it. She opened his jeans and slid her hand inside his briefs.

Sam gritted his teeth and pulled her close, trapping her hand. "You'd better slow down, sweetheart, or I won't be able to wait."

She wiggled her fingers against his erection. "I'm not prepared to wait."

"Then at least wait until I'm prepared." Sam set her away from him, groaning as she slowly withdrew her hand. He slipped off his shoes and shed the rest of his clothes.

Her eyes widened in anticipation. He was gorgeous. His hardened masculinity enticed her. She skimmed off her half-slip and kicked her shoes across the room.

Sam's tongue thrust into her mouth, mimicking the

action of his finger as it dipped inside her. He moaned when he encountered her heated wetness.

She clasped his shoulders, riding his hand. Frustrated and hungry for him, she leaned her body into his, then tipped him onto the bed, falling right next to him.

"Whoa." He laughed. "I get your message." With a grin, he reached for his pants on the floor and waved a foil packet at her.

After he opened it, she brushed his hands away to sheathe him. The power of his arousal excited her. She couldn't resist lingering over the task. He gritted his teeth as she caressed him. Unable and less than willing to wait, she pulled Sam on top of her. "We've had enough anticipation, don't you think?"

Sam gave her a smug grin. "I don't want to rush you."

"If you go any slower, I'm going to scream."

"That's the idea." As she guided him, he lowered his body onto hers. He pushed into her slowly, gritting his teeth.

Trish giggled, enjoying his torment as much as he'd enjoyed hers. "We can stop if you want."

"Oh, babe, I want all right. But stopping has nothing to do with it." He covered her lips with his.

Trish met his every thrust, energized by the magic of loving Sam. As her climax built, she hugged him tightly against her. Sharing love and making love. The glory of it overwhelmed her. She arched her back, pulling him closer with her hands on his buttocks, calling his name as she climaxed.

Her husky gasp burst his restraint. He thrust into her, meeting her demands and exceeding her hopes. She tumbled off the peak, secure that Sam tumbled right along with her.

Trish drifted back to consciousness, contented and smug. Cracking open an eye, she checked on Sam, tickled to see a sated grin on his face as well. His hand trailed over her shoulder, caressing its way down to settle on her breast.

"You were only half-right, you know," Sam said with a lazy grin. His dark blue eyes stirred the fires so recently banked. He made her feel beautiful and sexy.

"Half-right about what?"

"You implied you weren't going to be good anymore. I don't know if you consider that naughtier or nicer, sweetheart, but I do know one thing. If you keep it up, old Santa's gonna have a heart attack before he brings your presents."

"I don't care. I've already had my present."

"There could be more."

"How soon?" She laughed with Sam, delighted with their play. Humor and sex. She'd never experienced them together. Duke had viewed lovemaking a personal proving ground. Afterwards, he'd remind her of his endurance and his patience. His eye was always on the top of the mountain. Now she had a lover who took her to the top and held her hand while they jumped off together. With Sam, getting there was only half the fun.

"I've been wondering something all night," he said. "What the heck are maple bananas?"

Trish laughed and propped herself on her elbow. "Thinking of food already? I knew you had a sweet tooth, Sam Carrow."

He pulled her back into his arms and rolled her underneath him. "I only have a yearning to taste you."

They didn't get to the other dessert until much later.

*

Trish snuggled into the warmth of the bed, reluctant to awaken from the most blissful dream she'd ever had. Her body clock told her it was still before dawn. Warm breathing brushed her cheek. She wanted to slip back into her dream and relive her date.

Her eyes flew open as she stilled. Sam lay next to her, breathing across her cheek, warming her bed. Smiling at her with tenderness in his navy-blue eyes. She searched her mind for an appropriate "morning-after" attitude.

"Hi." The word squeaked out of her throat. Trish groaned to herself and offered him a small smile. She'd never had to face this awkward awakening. Although she and Duke had made love before their marriage, she hadn't fallen asleep with him until their honeymoon. She'd awakened to the comfort of their commitment to one another.

But she had no such guarantees in this situation. The gray pre-dawn light revealed too many of her insecurities. She could feel Sam watching her, although she found it difficult to meet his gaze. Staring at his luscious, clever mouth, Trish offered him another smile, this one less tentative as she recalled the wonderful feel of his lips on her body.

"Morning." Sam's watchfulness stretched her nerve endings. His still body portrayed his caution. Then he reached out and cupped her cheek, smoothing a strand of her hair back with his thumb. "Would it have been easier for you if I'd left in the dark?"

All her tension evaporated like fog in the heat of the sun. She smiled and curled her body closer into his. Her skin tingled and heated where it made contact with his hair-roughened firmness.

"I don't know when you would have snuck out." Recalling their night together, Trish gave him a wicked grin and watched his eyes widen. They'd made love several times, each more wonderful than the one before. The risqué jokes they shared over their maple banana dessert led to more tasting and pleasing and loving. "I seem to recall keeping you pretty busy."

He anchored her knee up over his hip. His hand roamed over her bottom, causing her to shiver. "That's very true. And I'm sure not complaining." He gazed steadily into her eyes. "But I can leave now if you want me to, so your neighbors don't see my car still parked out front."

Her heart filled with love at his thoughtfulness.

"I don't want to create problems for you. You mean too much to me." Sam drew a deep breath. "There's someplace I'd like to take you. I need to tell you a few things about myself."

"Oh, Sam." She smiled at him, feeling teary and oddly protective. There was virtually nothing he could tell her that would affect her feelings for him, but he was so sweet to worry. She took it as another sign that she'd become important to him.

He cleared his throat. He dropped his gaze, seeming uncomfortable. "It's about my house and why I have the time to fix it up right now."

"You don't have to tell me anything. Jenny told me all about that."

"There are things Jenny might have left out. Things I want to tell you in my own way."

She traced his chin with her forefinger. "Are you going to tell me you're involved with someone else?"

He jerked back with a frown. "No, of course not."

"Then nothing else matters." Trish lifted up on an elbow and stretched herself half over him. She put her heart into the kiss, soft, sweet yearning mixed with love. Sam's hands glided over her back and ribs. The kiss grew more heated, and her breath caught in raspy gasps. She skimmed her hand down his body and captured him, watching his eyes widen even as he grew hard against her palm. She gave him an arch look as she caressed him. "You still thinking of leaving?"

Sam smiled crookedly. "Not now."

"Good."

*

Trish eased out of bed, careful not to disturb Sam. The poor man needed his rest. She grinned, thinking of all the delicious things she'd love to spend the morning doing with him. Ty wasn't due back until after lunch. They had time for a leisurely breakfast, some more loving, and maybe a shower together.

A rush of anticipation shivered through her body. She grabbed the bedpost to steady herself, nearly dizzy with the strength of her feelings. She ran her gaze over Sam, rumpled and stubbly, gorgeous and utterly lovable. During the night, she'd committed herself to him, body and heart. Hopefully, Sam felt the same. If not, she'd just have to convince him. She couldn't imagine a life without Sam in it.

She pulled on a short satin robe. Knowing Sam would

see her in it, she felt wickedly decadent as the cool material slid against her nakedness. Belting it tightly, she tiptoed out to the hall. After a quick trip to the bathroom, she breezed into the kitchen, giddy at the thought of making breakfast for her lover. She hadn't felt this wonderful, ever. Perhaps with Duke, she'd been too young and then they'd fallen into a pattern. "Older and wiser" had its benefits.

When the doorbell rang, Trish jumped, dropping eggs in a runny mess from the countertop to the floor. *Who in the world?* She dashed toward the door before the bell woke Sam, loosening the belt on her robe so it would be less revealing. A quick check in the mirror assured her she didn't look indecent. She swung open the door.

Miriam stood on the porch, visibly shaking. Trish managed to draw half a breath. She tried to push back the instant guilt she felt faced with Duke's mother. Trish was less sure of herself than she needed to be for a confrontation with her mother-in-law.

"How could you?" Miriam stalked past her, looking around the living room, her eyes wild, her sharp face mottled. "I'm so angry, I can hardly stand to look at you."

"Miriam, please." Trish reached out a hand.

Miriam swatted it away. "Don't even think of touching me. This is *not* why we kept Tyler, so you could– I can't bear what you've done." Miriam spun away and gestured wildly toward the window. "I saw his car outside when I was coming home from the bakery. You can't deny that man's here."

Trish took another deep breath. Her house wasn't on Miriam's way home from the bakery, but her spying wasn't the issue just now. "I wasn't going to deny anything. If you'd just listen–"

"Listen? Listen? What could you possibly say to me that would erase what you've done? You've cheated on my son."

Trish stepped back, startled. "Duke is dead, Miriam."

"I'm well aware that my boy is gone. But you couldn't honor his memory, could you?" She sucked in a harsh breath.

Trish clenched her teeth and reined in her anger. She silently counted to ten before she spoke, reminding herself that this was Tyler's grandmother before her. "I don't appreciate the way you're talking to me, Miriam." Despite her efforts, her voice shook with anger. "Duke's been dead for four years. *Four years*. I never betrayed him, and I'll never forget him. But I'm a single woman now. I have a right to a life of my own."

Miriam thrust her face close, her steely eyes flat with bitterness. "Don't talk to me about your rights. You're a mother. You have a responsibility to my grandson. A judge might be interested to hear what you think you've got a right to do."

Trish schooled her voice into a quiet, even tone that

matched her deadly seriousness. "Miriam, I love you like my mother, otherwise I wouldn't have put up with your antics all these years. But I'm telling you this now. Don't ever challenge my fitness to raise Tyler."

They stared each other down. Trish braced herself for Miriam's next move.

"Who's at the door?" Sam called from the hall, his voice growing louder as he approached. He stumbled to a halt at the sight of Miriam, his mouth and eyes wide.

Trish might have laughed if she could have, but anger and fear ate away almost everything inside her. She saw the expressions chasing across Sam's face–surprise, embarrassment, then tense wariness as he took in their face-off. She registered the hatred vibrating off Miriam's body like a sonic boom, powerful but unseen, but Trish didn't feel any of it. She couldn't feel anything but the cold now seeping through her body.

Miriam glared at Sam, then stalked toward the door. "We didn't babysit Tyler so you could *entertain* a man."

The slam of the door didn't drown Sam's curse. He stalked after her. "How dare she–"

"Don't."

Sam whirled back and looked at her, confusion and anger visible on his face. "Don't what? Don't swear at her, or don't go after her?"

"Just don't." Anxiety gnawed at Trish.

He stepped toward her, stopping when she turned away. "What set her off?"

"It wasn't anything you did." Trish started when he clasped her hand. His touch nearly broke through the barrier protecting her. She needed distance, time to think this through. She eased her hand away. "Sam, would you mind if we didn't talk right now? Would you mind just going?"

"Honey, no. Talk to me. Let me help."

She faced him, shielded from feeling and absently grateful to be so. She didn't want to have to deal with anything. She only wanted Tyler, back in this house, back safe in her arms. Later, she'd have to consider the repercussions. What would she have to do to protect her son?

"Trish?"

"There's nothing you can do to help." She walked down the hall to her bedroom and closed the door with a tiny, deafening click.

*

Sam stalked through his house, too agitated to go to Bart and Jenny's. He only wanted to be with Trish, but she didn't want him. Obviously, she didn't need him.

He needed her, though. He needed her to tell him everything would be all right between them. He needed to try to help her, even if all he could offer was moral support.

He grabbed the sander, then thought better of it. The way he felt now, he'd wind up sanding the floor clear down to the basement. With more vigor than was necessary, he wound the cord back around the spindles on the handle, wishing for one moment he could wrap his hands around Miriam's neck.

A knock pulled him from his thoughts. The door opened and heavy footsteps pounded up the staircase.

"Hey, Sam," Bart called out. "Jenny sent me to remind you it's lunch time. You in the middle of something?" Bart walked into the bedroom-to-be.

"Yeah, I'm in the middle of a huge mess."

Bart looked around the room. "Looks like you're making real progress here."

Sam smiled, feeling no humor. "I meant the mess I'm making of my relationship with Trish."

Bart frowned and studied him. "What's wrong?"

Sam sighed and ran a hand through his hair, feeling the sweat he'd worked up. "You want a beer?"

"It's only noon, and it's Sunday. This must be bad." Bart led the way down the stairs. "What did you do?"

Sam opened the refrigerator door and pulled out two bottles. He offered one to Bart and smirked when Bart took it, despite his lecture upstairs.

"We were getting along fine. Uh, well, more than fine, if you know what I mean?"

Bart dropped onto his chair. "Spare me the details. I know what you mean."

Sam eyed his friend over the bottle as he drank. The malty flavor coated his tongue. "Maybe I shouldn't put you in the middle of this."

"It's okay. You're our best friends. Trish came to me as a client when her husband died. She and Jenny have been friends since Tyler started going to Jen's preschool."

"I planned to bring her over here today."

"Here?" Bart glanced around. "Why?"

Sam snorted. "It's a long story. Anyway, I walked into the front room to find her toe-to-toe with Miriam."

Bart groaned.

"I gather you know the woman."

"I've had the displeasure of her company once or twice," Bart said. "I can just imagine what she said to Trish."

"Then you're two steps ahead of me. When I got there, Miriam made a nasty insinuation about Trish *entertaining* me and slammed out."

Bart's chair legs hit the floor. "Where's Miriam get off acting like that?"

Sam raked his hair back in frustration. "Now Trish won't even talk to me."

"Women," Bart muttered.

"How can I fix this?"

"Call her."

"Didn't you hear what I said? She won't talk to me."

"Have you tried?"

"I'm telling you–"

"Have you tried?" Bart repeated with more force. Sam didn't answer. "That's what I thought. One thing I've learned from my marriage is you have to talk about your problems."

"You didn't see her expression." Sam ran a hand over his face. "What if she says it's over?"

"She's had time to think now. I'll go explain to Jenny that you're drinking your lunch."

Sam glowered. "Gee, thanks."

"Keeps her from trying to reform me."

Sam stared at his phone after Bart left. Even if Trish would talk to him, he didn't know what to say. He drummed his fingers on the table, thinking. Finally, it occurred to him. He didn't need to talk. He would listen, find out what happened, and just be supportive.

With a satisfied nod, he punched in the numbers. Maybe if things were better, he'd set up a date for her to come see his house. It was time–past time–to tell her the whole truth.

"Trish? It's Sam. I'm concerned about you." He listened

to silence for almost a full minute.

"I really can't talk right now."

He heard muffled noises and wondered if she was crying. His gut clenched, and he swallowed down the beer rising in his throat. "I'm coming over."

"No."

Sam waited, but she didn't say anything more. "Did Tyler get home all right?"

He distinctly heard her sob this time. He gripped the receiver. "Trish? Is Tyler okay?"

"He's fine." She cleared her throat and sniffed. "Jock brought him home."

"Did Jock say anything about me being there?"

"No. I'm not sure Miriam told him."

Sam blew out the breath he'd been holding. At least she hadn't been subjected to any more ugliness. He ached to be with Trish, to hold her in his arms and assure her everything was going to be fine. "When can I see you?"

"Oh, Sam, I don't know. I have some things to think through. I need to be alone. Please, try to understand."

"I'd like to, but there's more going on here than you're telling me. I can't help if I don't know what's wrong."

"I can't talk about it, Sam. Please."

"Will you call me if you need me? Promise me that much."

"I can't make any promises right now."

He didn't like the sound of that. He squeezed his eyes shut. "Well, I'm going to call you. Count on it." He waited to see how she'd respond, unwilling to let her push him away.

"All right," she said.

Sam blew out a relieved breath.

Now that he'd decided to clarify everything, the truth gnawed at his gut till he couldn't think straight. "Do you think you'll be up to seeing me later in the week?"

"I don't know. Maybe."

Sam swallowed hard. "Wednesday?"

"That's not the end of the week."

He smiled. "No, but it's later. How about it?"

"All right," she said softly and hung up the phone.

"All right!" Sam shouted into his empty house. He slapped a high-five onto the kitchen wall, then bounded up the steps. He had a lot of work to do before Wednesday.

*

Trish sighed as Tyler headed up the stairs at the McIntires' to play with Nick and Heather Wednesday evening. She followed Jenny into the kitchen. "I think he's glad to get away from me."

Jenny hung their coats in the mud room, then shut the door firmly. "Nonsense. Tyler adores you."

Trish slumped into a chair. "I've been too protective lately, but I'm going to let him sleep at Candy's Saturday. Her nephew's staying overnight, and she asked Ty, too. The four of them went camping over the summer and had such a great time." She gazed out the window over the sink. "I'm just paranoid about letting Tyler out of my sight."

Jenny set down two mugs of tea, then sat across the table from Trish. A line formed between her brows when she frowned. "Why? What's going on?"

"I have a problem."

"Does this have something to do with Sam?"

Trish stared into her mug. "Why would you ask that?"

"I haven't heard from you in a week. Sam's hardly ever here, and when he is, he walks around like he left his mind somewhere else. Or with someone else."

Trish glanced at Jenny. "This doesn't involve Sam. Well, only indirectly. I told him I needed some time alone to think about this problem."

"And he backed off? That doesn't sound like Sam. He's always trying to make everything better for everyone else." Jenny leaned forward. "He reminds me a lot of you."

"Another fixer?" Trish recalled sitting in this kitchen before Thanksgiving, blithely reassuring Jenny she'd take care of Miriam again this year, as she always did. Now the gods were punishing her overconfidence. She smirked at her naiveté.

"Believe me, the role is highly overrated."

"Considering your independent nature, I'm glad Sam's giving you some space."

"He's a nice man." Trish sipped her tea. She closed her eyes, relishing the mint flavor as its warmth spread through her.

"If you think he's so wonderful, what's the problem?"

"It isn't Sam." Trish propped her elbow on the table and let her cheek fall against her fist. "It's Miriam."

Jenny groaned. "I knew she'd try something."

"I think she wants custody of Ty."

Jenny gasped. "No! She can't. On what grounds?"

"She doesn't have any, which is why she's just threatening me right now. She claims I'm an unfit mother."

"That's ridiculous."

"I get sick just thinking how Ty will be affected, torn between me and his grandparents."

"Why would she even accuse you of being unfit?" As the silence stretched, Jenny's face went blank with astonishment. "Sam?"

Trish nodded.

"How'd she find out?"

Trish smiled ruefully. "You know my luck. Guess who came to the door Sunday morning, while Sam was looking all rumpled and cuddly."

Jenny winced. "Oh, no."

Trish shook her head. "Miriam's been driving past my house every couple of hours for the last three days."

"You're kidding."

"I've seen her. Then she calls me." Trish arched her eyebrow. "I won't tell you what she calls me since there are children in the house."

Jenny frowned. "She's accusing you of being unfit because you had a date with Sam?"

"Her friend, Lucille, is egging her on. But at some point, Miriam has to realize I'm not going to just let her have Tyler." Trish slumped in her seat. "I only hope she realizes it before she takes this any further. A legal battle, even over visitation rights, would destroy Tyler."

Jenny reached across the table and clasped Trish's hand. "What are you going to do?"

"I have to take her seriously, Jen, just in case." Trish's vision blurred. She blinked back tears. "Miriam might be bluffing, but I don't want to provoke her. She's so erratic right now, she might even run off with him. I just can't take any chances."

"Of course you can't. Do you want me to talk to Bart?"

Trish sighed. "I checked into possible problems after Duke died. Miriam has no grounds against me, but it's also against the law for me to interfere with a grandparent's visits."

"But you're not afraid of losing custody, right?"

Trish shook her head. "I worry about losing him, believe me, but it's not likely. I'm mostly worried about unsupervised visits, but if I stop them, she'll bring a case against me for sure."

"You don't think she'd hurt Ty."

"No. Not intentionally. The closet thing upset him and she had no idea. She just doesn't see anyone's point of view except her own. I'm a little worried she'd take off with him."

Jenny gaped. "I hadn't thought of that, but now that you've mentioned it, yeah, I can see it happening. She's really obsessed with Duke and therefore with Tyler."

"Exactly, but if I stay when Ty visits them, it might give her cause to charge me with interfering with their rights."

Jenny bit her lip. "Where does that leave your relationship with Sam?"

Trish shut her eyes against the sting of tears. "I don't know. I hope he'll wait for me to get through this, but I wouldn't blame him for hitting the road. My life is such a mess. I can't make him any promises right now."

"You'd let him go?"

"I may have to."

Jenny glowered and set her jaw.

Trish drew back, hurt by Jenny's reaction. Her throat clogged with unshed tears. "Don't look at me like that. Do you think I want to lose Sam? But if it comes to either that or risking Ty, there's no choice to make."

"I understand that. I just hate to see Miriam win."

Trish heard a thump. She dabbed her eyes and blew her nose. "I don't want Tyler to catch me crying. He already suspects something's wrong."

Jenny peered around Trish. "I can't imagine how he'll react, but maybe you should tell him."

"Are you crazy?"

"Are you talking about me?" a deep voice said behind Trish.

She spun toward the open door where Sam stood removing his jacket. He hung it on a peg, then smiled at her. "How am I going to react? To what?"

Trish opened her mouth, then closed it again. What could she say?

Sam shut the door and stepped toward her, leaving the smile behind. "Trish?"

She turned back to the table and blinked new tears from her eyes. "We weren't talking about you."

Jenny pushed back her chair. "I'll go check on the kids."

Trish stared, unable to believe Jen would abandon her. "You don't have to leave."

Sam came around the table and sat on the chair between them. He glanced from Trish to Jenny and back. "What makes me think our date's off?"

Trish gasped and covered her mouth. Embarrassment washed over her cheeks.

"You forgot."

"Oh, Sam, I feel terrible."

He clasped his warm hand over hers and squeezed it. "Don't worry about it. It looks like something else has happened."

Jenny leaned forward. "He doesn't know?"

Trish grimaced.

"Do you think that's fair?" Jenny stood. "This concerns him, too."

Trish soaked in the sight of Sam as Jenny left the room. "She's right. I'm sorry. I just need time to figure out what to do."

"I might be able to help."

She withdrew her hand from his and crossed her arms, feeling the cold irony in her chest. She'd finally found an honest, supportive man, and she'd have to give him up to protect her son.

How could she explain this without hurting him? "I don't know how to tell you."

"Just say it. Is Miriam upset because you're seeing me?"

"Yes." She hugged herself tightly. The cold wouldn't go away. "She wants Tyler."

Sam's mouth dropped open. He jumped to his feet. "What? She can't do that." He stopped suddenly, a frown etched into his face. "Can she?"

"I hope not."

Sam paced the length of the kitchen. "Have you talked to anyone? A lawyer? What does Bart say?"

"I haven't gone to a lawyer yet."

"Why not? For Pete's sake, Trish, you've got to do something." Sam raked his hand through his hair, leaving it spiked. He let out an exasperated huff and paced across the kitchen again.

After a moment, he dropped onto Jenny's chair across from her and rubbed his face with his palms. He shook his head. "See what a help I can be?"

She smiled a little, knowing her news had shocked him into the outburst. "I understand."

"Sorry I blew up like that." His breath whistled out through his teeth. "Doing nothing goes against the grain, but I'm sure you have a good reason."

"I'm trying not to antagonize Miriam. If I go into Bart's office, I'm afraid she'll counter with a lawyer of her own."

"How would she know where you're going?" Sam's

sharp eyes pierced her. "Is she having you followed?"

"No." Trish decided not to add that Miriam did her own surveillance. "I talked to Bart about my rights when Duke died. At the time, Miriam wanted us to move in with them."

Sam shuddered.

"My feelings exactly. When I wouldn't agree, she offered to raise Ty for me, saying how she needed him."

"So this has been going on for four years?"

"On and off. Bart reassured me that grandparents can't take a child without cause, but I'd still rather not provoke Miriam."

"Do you think it would get as far as the courts?"

Trish hesitated. She didn't want to worry him with her fears of Miriam just up and running away with Tyler. "Probably not, but the legal system isn't perfect. All it would take is one judge who didn't like the way his grandchild was being raised, or who never got to see him, and I'd be sunk. Frankly, the idea of a court case scares me senseless."

He nodded. "You know Miriam best."

"Unfortunately, I do."

Sam leaned toward her. "Is it because you're seeing me? Is our relationship causing problems for you?"

She couldn't stand the turmoil darkening his eyes. If she downplayed the situation, it would protect Sam's feelings. "I'm half-convinced this will all blow over after Christmas. If I can keep her calm one more week, it'll be okay."

"You really think so?"

She nodded. "Miriam gets emotional every year. Duke's birthday and the anniversary of his death are bad, but Christmas is the worst It's classic holiday depression." She bit her lip. "I'm sorry I forgot our date."

"It's okay. You've had a few things on your mind."

His understanding almost broke her heart. Barely able to draw a breath, she waited for him to ask his next question. She could guess what it would be, but she didn't want to answer.

"How about a rain check?" he asked.

Trish blinked back tears. "I can't. I'm just going to lie low for a while."

Sam looked away, a muscle pulsing in his cheek. She couldn't think of a thing to say to make the situation better. The silence smothered her like wet wool on a warm day. Sam slipped farther away from her with each tick of the kitchen clock.

She rose. "I'm sorry."

He studied her with little furrows around his blue eyes. A sharp pain pierced her at the anguish reflected there.

"I understand you're doing what you think is best," he said in a gruff tone. "But, remember, you have no reason to feel guilty."

Trish grabbed her coat. Turning, she almost bumped into Jenny. "I have to go. I'll come back for Ty in a couple of hours."

"Wait." Jenny grabbed her sleeve. She darted a look at Sam, who stared steadily at Trish. Jenny rocked back on her heels, seeming to change her mind regarding what she'd planned to say. "What about our party Saturday night?"

"Don't count on me." Trish rushed out the door.

Sam jolted as the door closed behind her.

"What happened?" Jenny asked. "Didn't she tell you what's going on?"

"She told me."

"Well? Aren't you going to help her fight Miriam?"

Sam snorted. "That's exactly what I'd like to do, but Trish doesn't want to fight Miriam. She's running scared, like a rabbit chased by a wolf." He shook his head. "I can't blame her. She can't risk losing Tyler. She has to choose him over me."

"Oh, Sam, it's not like that."

"It feels exactly like that."

Jenny dropped onto a chair. "I don't know how Trish should handle her. Miriam's so unpredictable."

Sam gave her a dark look. "I can think of some ways I'd like to handle Miriam."

Jenny sat up straight. "I know you're kidding, but don't even call her, Sam. You must have some idea how she'd react."

"I know." He growled in this throat, the frustration eating at him. "This is crazy. One malicious old woman has Trish cowering in her house, afraid to make a wrong move for fear of losing her son. Now I'm going to lose them both."

CHAPTER ELEVEN

When the phone rang Saturday afternoon, Trish expected the caller to be Candy, finalizing plans for Tyler's overnight stay.

"Hello, Trish, dear."

Miriam. Trish drooped against the wall. "Hello."

"I was just saying to Jock how nice it would be for Tyler to come over for dinner. Shall we pick him up in half an hour?"

How like Miriam to call and demand she serve up Ty on a moment's notice. Miriam probably believed Trish would be intimidated by her threats and give in to anything.

"Miriam, I asked you a few weeks ago if you'd like to keep Ty tonight. You turned me down."

The line fell silent for a moment. "I believe I asked for a different date, dear. I would certainly never turn away an opportunity to see my grandson."

Miriam's reasonable tone caught her off-guard. Was someone with Miriam, coaching her? Someone like Lucille? Trish wouldn't put it past Miriam to record the call, so she could show a judge how fair-minded she could be. Trish shook off her paranoia.

"Besides," Miriam continued, "a boy should be able to sleep in his own bed. We'll bring Tyler back after we've eaten."

Trish gritted her teeth, knowing Miriam referred to Ty being gone when Sam had come to dinner. And stayed. She decided to let the remark pass. "I'm sorry, Ty has other plans."

"Oh? Are you taking him someplace?"

To the other side of the planet, away from you. Trish bit her cheek. She might as well tell her. She didn't need Miriam parking down the street in her sunglasses and trench coat all night.

"He's spending the night with Candy." Her pulse pounded against her temple as she waited for Miriam's reply.

"I presume you have plans, as well," Miriam said in an acid tone. "Plans that chase your son from his own house."

Trish clenched her jaw, determined not to be drawn by Miriam's vile bait. "You may presume what you please, Miriam. You will, anyway."

The phone crashed in Trish's ear. Sick to her stomach, Trish cursed herself for her impulse. Had she just provoked Miriam into action?

*

"Please," Trish said to Candy in her living room fifteen

minutes later, "don't let Ty out of your sight." She raised her hand to stop Candy's interruption. "I know you're always careful with him, especially in public. But he'd go off with Miriam or Jock without thinking, no matter what I tell him. And what can I tell him? She hasn't done anything yet."

Trish glanced down the hall where she could hear Ty playing with Candy's nephew, Billy.

"We'll call in the pizza." Candy nodded. "I'll take care of him, don't worry."

"I know you will. He needs to get away from me and have some fun."

"Don't be so hard on yourself. You're holding up well. I'd have killed Miriam by now."

Trish smiled slightly. "No, you wouldn't."

"Don't be too sure. I may do it, anyway, for how she's treating you."

Trish sank back on the sofa with a sigh. "I don't care what she says to me, as long as Ty doesn't hear it. I can't trust her with him right now."

"You just concentrate on Tyler. I'll take care of him tonight and the store tomorrow."

"I should be worrying about business. I should plan more sales to bring in customers." Even thought of expending all that energy right now made Trish tired.

Candy rubbed her stomach. "Hanging those custom-ordered quilts on the walls as you finished each one was brilliant. They appealed to a lot of customers, and the ladies who commissioned them strutted around like peacocks. You'll probably have double the orders next Christmas."

"Twice the work?" Trish eyed Candy. "Is this your way of cheering me up?"

Candy grinned. "Speaking of quilts, did you finish Sam's? Can I see it?"

Trish brought it out for Candy. Handling it awakened Trish's dreams of a future with Sam. Her heart ached, and she had to swallow hard.

"It's beautiful," Candy cried, spreading it beside her on the couch. "You didn't happen to take pictures of it before you changed it, did you?"

"No, why?"

"I just thought we could display the before and after shots in the store. Showcase your talent and show people what's possible."

Trish laid her hand on Candy's shoulder. "Thank you. Both for the compliment and the strategy planning." She smiled. "If I weren't the owner, I'd say you deserve a raise."

Candy smiled wryly. "Gee, thanks. I'll remember you almost said that at review time. And don't worry. I'll think of something to boost January sales other than White-material

Sales."

"Mom." Tyler ran down the hall toward them, with Billy on his heels. "Can I take my camping gear?"

"Whatever for?"

"Me and Billy want to put up Candy's tent in their basement." He turned to Candy. "Is it okay?"

Candy shrugged. "Fine by me."

Tyler's expression lit with hope. "Mom?"

"Sure, tiger. Unless, of course, you'd want to stake it outside in the snow."

"Aw, Mom." He ran off, while Billy trailed behind.

"It's easy to see which one's the mischief-maker."

"Don't dismiss the quiet one," Candy said. "Billy's shy, but he's devious. He's too quick for me to keep up with. I hope my kid's just as precocious." Candy rubbed her bulging tummy again.

"I'm sorry I'm distracted right now." Trish folded the quilt. "It's funny. Owning Fancy Fabrics was my dream for so many years. Becoming independent was my driving goal after Duke died. Now the store seems so unimportant."

"You'll snap out of it as soon as Miriam backs down. And she will, just as she always does, right after her Christmas blues go away."

"I'm banking my future on it."

Candy nodded. "Sam will love this quilt."

Trish looked away.

"What? Don't tell me something happened with Sam?"

"Not exactly. We're just not seeing each other right now."

"Right now? As in, you've broken it off until after Christmas?"

She nodded, unable to meet Candy's eyes.

"Trish, you can't do that."

"You don't understand," she pleaded. "What am I supposed to do? Tell Miriam to go ahead and do her worst? You don't know Miriam's worst. I can't risk hurting Ty."

"What you can't do is give in to Miriam. You're acting like you're guilty of something. Do you think it's wrong to find happiness with Sam?"

"Of course not."

"Is Sam not good enough for you? Is he another user like Duke?"

"Sam would never intentionally hurt anyone."

"Then why are you letting Miriam win?"

Trish glanced down the hall. Tyler and Billy were whooping like wild things. They couldn't possibly overhear the conversation. "I only care about protecting Ty."

"I understand that. But why does protecting Tyler mean you have to lose Sam?"

Anguish twisted Trish's heart. "I hope I don't."

Candy huffed. "Okay. Say he waits for you until Miriam backs off. When things are calm, you'll start seeing Sam again. Suppose Miriam objects? What are you going to do? Give him up again?"

Trish didn't have an answer.

"When you met Sam, you didn't want to be attracted to him because you thought he might be a manipulator. You didn't want to lose your independence to him." Candy struggled off the couch with a scowl. "What do you think's going on now? Except it isn't Sam who's pulling your strings."

Candy stalked down the hall, calling, "Tyler, Billy. Time to go."

Alone again, Trish pulled Sam's quilt from its box and took it downstairs to the TV room. She turned on a small table lamp and eased back into her rocking chair, pulling the quilt around her. She didn't want to lose Sam. She loved him. But Sam would survive without her. Tyler needed her.

Trish rocked in the chair, letting her mind wander. She pulled the quilt up to her cheek. This was all she'd ever have of Sam, and it wasn't even his. He'd never seen it, let alone slept under it. She wouldn't have the comfort of his scent to curl up with. Sam had no idea the quilt existed, that she'd labored over it, binding it with thread and dreams. Without Sam to share it, the quilt would provide her with only physical warmth.

Trish pushed against the floor with her foot, setting the chair rocking again. The house hummed around her, louder than she'd ever noticed. Too loud. And too quiet. Maybe she'd get a cat to wander around and meow and curl up in her lap. Her grandmother had had a cat–three, actually. Trish could picture herself, old and gray, in this rocker, with this quilt and a house full of cats.

She stopped rocking. "A cat? I don't want a cat," she said to the empty room. "I want Sam."

She jumped to her feet, leaving the chair rocking madly. Gathering the quilt in her arms, she rushed upstairs.

"A cat," she muttered darkly. Furious with herself, Trish refolded the quilt, snapping the corners briskly, then shoved it back into its box none too gently. She checked the time. Nine o'clock. Tyler was safe with Candy. Sam would still be at Jenny and Bart's party. She charged down the hall to her room. Leaning on the vanity table, she glared into the mirror.

"You should be ashamed of yourself," she told her reflection. "As hard as you fought for your independence, and now you're letting Miriam run your life? Miriam? It would serve you right if you did end up with a cat." She growled in frustration and turned her back on that pathetic creature in the mirror.

Miriam's insecurity and implied threats had paralyzed

Trish with fear, but she'd learned her lesson. Her father had manipulated her, Duke had manipulated her, but, by God, she wouldn't let Miriam manipulate her.

After applying a smattering of makeup and brushing out her hair, she dressed rapidly, pulling on a knee-length, full-skirted, red knit dress from the closet. Facing the mirror, Trish did a quick check. She looked confident. Adrenaline pumped through her body, adding energy to her determination. No court in the land would take her son from her. She was an exemplary mother. As for her relationship with Sam, falling in love wasn't illegal. She was a healthy and responsible woman who planned to build a future.

Trish marched out of the room to claim her man.

*

Sam eased himself away from the crowd in Bart and Jenny's living room. The room full of people underscored his loneliness. He let himself into Bart's study and dialed Trish. He knew she wouldn't come to the party. He just wanted to hear her voice and make sure she was okay.

The phone rang several times. Either Trish wasn't home or she wasn't picking up. Disappointed, he wandered back to the party.

Fingernails dug into his forearm. "Hey, good looking."

Sam stopped. The low-pitched voice in his ear issued the

right invitation, but it was the wrong voice. Jenny's nineteen-year-old niece smiled up at him and batted her eyelashes playfully. Andrea's brown eyes shone with innocence and hope. Her smooth olive skin was flushed with good cheer and, judging by her fruity breath, too much wine. Sam shook his head.

"Don't say no," Andrea said. "You don't even know what I want yet."

Neither do you, he wanted to tell her. He let her pull him a few steps closer to the kitchen. "I hesitate to ask, but what do you want?"

"Just this." She glanced over their heads.

Sam did likewise. Spotting the mistletoe, he frowned down at her. "You're trouble."

Andrea grinned. "Why, thank you. That's the nicest compliment a man's ever given me."

"Sorry. I'm spoken for."

"Really?" She looked on either side of him. "I don't see anyone here who'd object."

"I'd object," a voice said behind him.

Sam spun around, his heart thudding with disbelief and hope.

"Hello, Sam." Trish's gaze shifted to Andrea. "And you are?"

"Having rotten luck tonight." Andrea patted his arm.

"See ya."

He hardly noticed her leaving while he absorbed the sight of Trish. She glided toward him, her red dress swirling around her legs. His mouth went dry and his mind blank.

"You're right where I want you," she said.

"I am?"

She pointed at the mistletoe, then closed the distance. "Merry Christmas, Sam." She pulled down his head as she rose to kiss him.

His galloping heartbeat eased into a steady rhythm. By no means was he calm, but the relief of having Trish come to him, the pleasure of holding her in his arms, settled his emotions. Everything would work out. Finally.

Sam covered her mouth with his. He wanted to devour her, to make her a part of him. He kissed her with the force of his passion, with his heart full of love.

Cheers and applause rang around them, and they jerked apart. Trish gasped as her cheeks turned bright pink. Sam smiled and tried to slow his breathing. He regarded the crowd around them. Bart, grinning widely, led the ovation.

"Thank you," Sam said. "Show's over." He grabbed Trish's hand and headed for the door. Their audience voiced a teasing protest but parted to let them through.

Scanning the crowded driveway, Sam growled in his

throat, frustrated to have gotten out of the house, only to be tossed another obstacle. "My car's blocked in."

Trish giggled and pointed down the street, loving his eagerness. "Mine's not."

Once at her house, they could barely keep their eyes off each other. She felt as though she were filled with helium, floating, and loving the sensation.

"I have something to tell you," Sam said.

The doorbell rang.

He swore. "I'm going to disconnect that thing."

Trish read the sudden anxiety in his eyes as he turned toward her.

"Do you think–?" Sam began.

Trish burst out laughing. The situation was too absurd not to laugh. "Of course it's Miriam. That woman has radar where I'm concerned. Sam, I'd like to see her alone."

He spun toward her, his expression tight with refusal. "We should face this together. We're a couple, right?"

"Of course we are." Trish laid her cheek against his chest where his heart beat strongly. "And you can be my backup next time. But I need to prove to Miriam that she can't push me around."

The muscles in his cheek bulged as he clenched his teeth. The doorbell rang once again. Trish kissed a path along his rigid jawline.

Sam's knees buckled. "Five minutes."

"You're an angel." Prepared for battle, she hurried to the front room and swung open the door to face–

"Jock," she gasped. Her face went cold as the blood drained away.

"You expected Miriam."

Trish nodded. She noticed the heightened color in Jock's face and thought he was angry. Then she realized that his gaze never met hers as he inspected the door frame, the porch boards, even her mailbox. She waved him in.

Jock glanced inside. He appeared as nervous as a Roman slave approaching the arena full of lions.

"What can I do for you?"

"Nothing. I'm the one who should..." He turned away.

Trish regarded him with surprise. He paced off, then back to her. She only just stopped herself from stepping backward in self-defense. Jock's tormented expression revealed his churning emotions.

"It's Miriam," he said. "She came home last night after driving past here. She came in ranting about you." He grabbed Trish's hands in his cold ones. She started and had to steady herself to keep from recoiling. His eyes bore into hers. "I swear to you, Trish, I had no idea she'd been doing any of this. I just now heard the whole story."

Trish shook her head. Jock, emotional and rambling. She had to gather her wits.

"You must believe me. I had no idea." Jock gathered her into his arms. "You're the daughter of my heart. I'd never let anyone hurt you."

Relief swept through her. She thought she'd lost him. She sniffed and wiped her eyes with her fingertips. "What do we do now?"

"That's up to you. I don't want to lose you or Tyler, but I'd understand if you didn't want to see us."

"Tyler would miss you terribly. And so would I." She hesitated, unable to phrase her thoughts.

He sighed heavily. "But there's Miriam."

"Yes."

Jock slumped onto the couch. He tipped his head and regarded the ceiling. "Did I ever tell you why I nicknamed my son Duke?"

Trish perched on a chair, surprised at the change of subject and the question. Everyone knew the story. "You liked John Wayne, and Duke liked to pretend he was a cowboy."

Jock smiled and shook his head. "That's just what I told everybody. I really did it to protect him."

"Protect him?"

Jock waved a hand. "Maybe that's the wrong word. I wanted to give him strength. He already had a pansy name to deal with. Elliott, for God's sake!"

Trish swallowed a chuckle.

"When Duke was born, his blood type didn't match with Miriam's, and he had to have a total transfusion. We were afraid he would die, no matter how often the doctors reassured us."

"I've never heard this before."

"We don't like to talk about it. I've never prayed so much in my life. I would have let her name the kid Wimpy, which is practically what she did."

Trish laughed. "So, he got stuck with an unusual name. Elliott isn't really so bad."

"I could have lived with the name. But we were advised against having more children, and Miriam suffocated the boy with love. He was turning into a whiny mama's boy. So I nicknamed him Duke and starting doing more masculine things with him, like fishing and playing ball."

Trish suppressed a smile, knowing he was teasing her to break the tension. "Girls fish and play ball."

"Don't sidetrack me with a feminist lecture." Jock grinned. "You know what I'm saying."

Trish sobered. "Yes, I do. You saved your son."

"And I'll do no less for my grandson." He regarded her steadily. "I thought I'd take Miriam on some long weekend trips after Christmas. Use up some of my vacation."

Trish swallowed the tears in her throat. A movement caught her attention as Sam joined them. He stopped in the middle of the room, legs spread in an aggressive stance, and eyed the man on the couch. Trish sighed softly. Her knight had come to her rescue.

"Sir." He tipped his head in a stiff, polite gesture.

Jock smiled benignly. "Son."

Sam loosened his rigid stance. A warm glow of love swept through her. He was exceptional, ready to fight her battles, yet giving her the opportunity to deal with them herself first. How'd she get so lucky to find such an honorable, gallant man?

"Well." Jock clapped his hands onto his knees in a gesture of finality before he rose. "I'll get out of your way. Will you let Tyler come over Christmas night?"

Trish hesitated. Even with Jock's support, the idea unnerved her. His shoulders slumped, and Trish realized he might read her hesitation as a lack of trust. Not able to deny it, she linked her hand through his arm. "Why don't you and Miriam spend Christmas Day here? My family's coming and we'd love for you to join us."

"You're sure?"

"Positive."

Jock engulfed her in his typical bear hug. A tremor

passed through him before he released her.

"Thank you," Jock said.

"No." She held his gaze with hers. "Thank you."

Sam's arms came around her from behind as she watched Jock walk to his car. She leaned back and let Sam support her, feeling warm and loved.

"What happened?" he asked.

"He just found out what Miriam's been up to. He didn't know." Her voice caught as tears clouded her vision. She waved goodbye as Jock pulled away. "He didn't know."

Sam shut the door, then turned her in his arms. He rocked her and stroked his hand soothingly over her hair.

After a minute, Trish smiled up at him. "I'm so relieved. Jock means a lot to me and it hurt to think he'd be party to this. But he wasn't. As soon as he found out, he stopped Miriam."

"That's great. Do you think he can keep Miriam in line? He didn't strike me as being particularly in-charge before."

"I know. But Jock's a strong man, and now he's motivated to curb Miriam's obsession with Duke." She shrugged. "It won't happen overnight, but I think she'll overcome it with Jock's help."

Joy filled her. She threw her arms around Sam's neck and kissed him exuberantly. "Oh, Sam. Everything's so perfect now. I haven't been this happy in a long time."

An odd look crossed Sam's face. Her stomach tightened as she braced herself for bad news. "Sam?" She pulled back to look at him. His smile strained his features. "What is it?"

"It's time you saw my house."

CHAPTER TWELVE

Trish sagged with relief. "We've been through this. It doesn't matter. I love you." She cupped his face in her palms and stressed each word. "I. Love. You."

Sam closed his eyes and pressed her hands tighter. "I love you, too, Trish. These past days have been hell."

His gentle kiss worried rather than reassured her.

"You might want to put on something warmer. It's cold at my place." He sounded resigned to face whatever came rather than excited about their future.

Trish went to her room and changed into a sweatshirt and black jeans. When she returned to the living room, she found Sam pacing. She shook her head at him and picked up their coats. "When are you going to believe in me, and in us, as a couple?"

She held his hand as he drove to reassure him with her touch. His house must be pretty run down for him to be so nervous about her reaction. Trish rehearsed polite ways to assure him it didn't matter what his house looked like. They could raze the place and live in her house. As the silence stretched, his lack of belief in her started to grate on Trish. "Did you fall in love with me because of my house?"

Sam threw her a startled glance, then his expression flattened. "It's not the same thing."

"Of course it is. If you don't love me because of what I have, why would I stop loving you because of what you don't have?"

He groaned. "Honey, I know you mean well, but you're not making this any easier."

She grimaced and turned toward the side window. They passed through a nice neighborhood, newer than hers by about thirty years. Large houses sat on half-acre lots. Trish smiled at one house decked out in whimsical teddy bear Santas. Every surface of the house next to it twinkled, covered with thousands of Christmas lights.

Had Sam chosen this route to illustrate the difference between them? To show her what he could never give her? She shook her head at his obstinate integrity.

Sam turned into a grander, more expensive extension of the subdivision. Trish frowned, not recalling a through street. Where was he going? Three turns later, Sam pulled her car into a driveway. A beautiful, two-story brick with a dozen windows stood back from the street, fronted by a huge, professionally landscaped yard.

"Why are we stopping?"

He clenched his jaw, then turned. His eyes searched hers. "This is my house."

She started to smile at his joke, but it froze on her cheeks. She glanced back at the house. New, it would have cost over half a million dollars. It wasn't five years old.

He opened his car door, and she followed woodenly. Even if the inside was a wreck, it wouldn't have been come cheap. The tiled foyer opened into a formal living room, which turned into a huge dining room, with French doors leading onto an enclosed deck. A battered dinette, similar to hers, clashed with the shiny efficiency of the stainless steel appliances.

Unable to form a coherent thought, Trish followed him. The smells of recently sawn wood, fresh paint, and new carpet suffocated her. She glanced in the den just long enough to note the desk with a fax machine sitting by the computer and a drafting table situated under a double-wide window. She wasn't surprised to find the powder room bigger than her only bathroom at home. She wasn't surprised by anything.

She was in shock.

Sam stopped at the bottom of the beautifully carved oak staircase, his expression the epitome of guilt and apprehension. Ignoring him, Trish dragged herself up the steps, her feet as heavy as her heart. Five bedrooms, each larger than the last, graced the upstairs. Sawhorses sat in one; new drywall had been hung in another. Three full bathrooms and another powder room mocked her.

She turned to study him. "Who are you?"

"I own Scarecrow Construction."

Her mouth dropped at the name of the largest construction company in the area, and beyond. S. Carrow. Scarecrow. She'd never have connected the two. She'd certainly never have connected Sam with the multi-millionaire owner of the construction company. He'd hidden the truth too artfully, orchestrating every conversation, building on her misconception.

She felt like a fool.

"This house needed a lot of work. I was going to resell it for a profit in the spring. That's how I've made a lot of my money. But the market isn't promising, and since meeting you, I've been thinking of keeping it."

Trish ignored the hope in his eyes. "A lot of your money?"

He thrust his hands in his pockets and hunched his shoulders. "The company's done pretty well. I also have some rental properties."

Trish eyed him steadily. He still wasn't telling her the whole truth. She swallowed to erase the sense of betrayal in her mouth. "So, what are you worth? A few million?"

"What difference does it make? I'm the same man."

She shook her head. "I don't even know you."

"That's not true."

The scoffing denial that rose from her throat sounded loud in the echoing stillness. "Well, you'd know all about what's not true, wouldn't you? You've lied to me from the beginning."

She stalked across the floor, too agitated to stand still, too heart-sore to face him. "I'll bet you laughed your head off when I hired you as a handyman."

"It wasn't like that."

She spun to face him. "No? Then tell me how it was, Sam. Tell me how you corrected me when I hired you, thinking you needed the job. Tell me how you admitted you were a multi-millionaire–although I'm pretty sure I would have remembered hearing that."

"Okay, okay. I didn't tell you right off. I wanted someone who wanted me rather than my money. When you didn't know who I was, it seemed like a blessing."

"I'll just bet. Why didn't you tell me?"

"Women are attracted by the money. You even said you want to marry a rich man."

"When did I ever say such a thing?"

"In your kitchen, when you hired me."

She scowled.

He rushed on. "Jenny told me the same thing the first night I met you."

"Jenny? Just what did she say?"

"She said you needed a rich husband."

Trish gave him an eye roll. "Of course I do. Every woman does. That doesn't mean I'd marry a man just for his money. Is that what you think of me?"

"Not now that I've gotten to know you."

She threw her hands in the air and turned away.

"Before I met you, I had trouble believing. When I found out the kind of woman you are, warm and loving, and honest and special, I was afraid to lose you."

Her arms folded over her chest, trying to hold in the ache, she voiced her deepest pain. "You manipulated me."

"Never."

She whirled toward him. "Right from the beginning and up till a few minutes ago."

"I know you're surprised." Sam frowned when she snorted at his understatement. "But after you get used to the idea, it's really not so bad, is it?" He raised his hands, palms up. "It could have been a lot worse, like I was married or an axe-murderer. But that's not the problem." He smiled. "I just have money."

Trish slumped against the wall, her mouth hanging open. "You just don't get it, do you? It isn't the money. It's you. You're a stranger." She held up her hand as Sam started to interrupt. "The Sam I knew was honest and caring. You only told me what you wanted me to know. Why couldn't you have trusted me?"

He took a deep breath. "I admit I should have told you sooner. I was wrong."

She stared at him. "That's it? You were wrong? Everything's all right now?"

He thrust his fists in his pockets. "Obviously not."

"Obviously not," she echoed hollowly. "I can't trust you anymore."

The color drained from his face.

"I can't have another relationship with a man I can't trust. I can't live my life wondering if you're telling me the truth, or if you're just telling me what you want me to know." *Like Duke did.* She shook off the thought. "It would destroy me. It would destroy us." She turned away.

"Trish, don't leave. There's got to be a way we can get through this. I love you. I'm sorry. Let me fix it."

Trish couldn't bear to look at him. She couldn't bear the pain. She swallowed hard. "Goodbye, Sam." She ran from his house.

Trish drove to Jenny's to pick up Ty the next Tuesday. She'd only had one call from Sam, which was a blessing. As much as her heart ached, it was over. He had deceived her. She'd never trust him not to manipulate her. No matter how she'd tried to understand his side of it, she just couldn't believe in him.

She'd discussed Miriam and Jock's upcoming trips with Tyler, but Sam's departure from their lives hadn't been mentioned. Ty spent a good deal of time at Nick's, but he didn't talk about what he did there. With Christmas just a few days away, she hoped his silence reflected only holiday secrets.

Although now that Trish thought of it, during Sam's call earlier, Ty had hopped from foot to foot, reaching for the phone. When she told Sam nothing had changed and hung up without letting Ty speak to him, he had sulked off to his room. Moments later, Jenny called to ask if he could come play with Nick and Heather. Ty's eyes lit with relief, but he wouldn't meet his mother's gaze for long. She'd assumed he felt embarrassed by his sulking, but perhaps he missed Sam more than she'd supposed he would.

Trish parked in the driveway and took a deep breath. She didn't want to see Sam, remembering her dreams for the future with him that would never come true now.

When no one answered the door, she walked around to

the backyard. She heard Sam's voice in the garage and stopped short.

"You have to clean the paintbrushes, tiger, or they'll dry out and you won't be able to use them next time."

Trish caught her breath. "Tiger" was her nickname for Tyler.

"I remember," Ty said. "We use this turpertiny stuff."

"Turpentine. Or water, if there's not a grown-up around."

"Okay. Hey, Sam." Ty's voice sounded hesitant.

Sam? Not Mr. Carrow? She insisted Ty address adults with respect, not as peers. He'd probably asked permission from Sam to use his first name. They'd become closer than she realized.

"Yeah?"

"Do you think it's okay not to tell Mom about us doing this?"

"Do you think your mom would be upset that we're together?"

"No, but she asks me about playing with Nick and Heather, and I feel real bad 'cause I'm really working with you, not playing. But it's her Christmas present, so I can't tell her. Do you think it'll be okay after she opens the bird feeder?"

"Yeah, it's okay to keep a Christmas secret. But any other time, when it's not a present, you should always be honest."

"I learned that when I dropped Horsey in the toilet. Mom wouldn't have been so mad at me if I'd told her right away."

"You're smarter than I am, Ty. Sometimes we have to learn the hard way that it's better to tell the truth, no matter if we think we'll get in trouble."

"Did you ever get in trouble, Sam?"

Trish peeked around the corner of the garage, unable to resist seeing Sam's face. He had squatted down beside Tyler. Now he reached out and ruffled Ty's hair, but the faint smile he gave Tyler appeared strained.

"Not telling the truth makes trouble for all of us, no matter how old we get. Now, go on in and wash your hands. Mrs. McIntire will be back soon to take you home."

Trish ducked back around the side of the garage so Ty wouldn't see her as he passed. As soon as the house door slammed, she stepped out into the open.

Sam jerked as though he'd been slapped. After a moment, he turned back to Bart's workbench. "Act surprised on Christmas. Tyler's worked hard on this."

She cleared her throat. "It was nice of you to help him, considering everything."

He pinned her with a scorching glare. "Whatever else you may think of me, I hope you know I'd never disappoint Tyler."

She hesitated, not knowing what to say. She wanted to say she believed him, but the words wouldn't come.

"Forget it." Disgust etched his features before he stalked away from her.

Her chest tightened, but how could she agree Sam was an honorable man? She had proof to the contrary. Believing without proof was an act of faith. Believing when the proof indicated otherwise was a leap of faith she couldn't risk.

*

After a quick walk around the block which did nothing to ease his frustration, Sam plodded up the steps to the deck and sank into a chair. Warm sunlight flooded the deck. Elbows planted on his knees, he rubbed his face. Feminine voices wafted from the open kitchen window.

"Why would you need Bart?" he heard Jenny ask. "Isn't Sam playing you-know-who?"

Sam leaned closer to the window.

"He was," Trish replied. "But we aren't seeing each other anymore."

"So I've heard." Jenny's acerbic tone had a cutting edge.

"He told you?"

"It wasn't hard to guess, but yes, he told us. He didn't say why, though."

The silence from inside drove Sam to his feet. Peering in

through the screen, he could just make out Jenny's expression of interest and concern. Trish sat with her back to him.

Trish shrugged, or perhaps she shifted uncomfortably under Jenny's sharp eye. He wished he could see her face.

"Sam lied to me," she said.

"That doesn't sound like him."

"He let me believe something without correcting my mistake."

"You made a mistake, so you've shut out the best man I've ever known, other than Bart?"

Sam grinned at the compliment.

Jenny went on. "How is this Sam's fault? What was it you misunderstood?"

Trish squirmed. "I thought he was poor."

"What?"

"You heard me."

Jenny hooted. "Sam Carrow has more money than Bart and I will ever see, unless we hit the Lotto jackpot." She stilled. "Is that the problem? You think he'll control you because he came into the relationship with more money?"

"That hadn't occurred to me."

Sam rolled his eyes. *Thanks, Jenny.* He didn't need another obstacle.

Trish continued, "But Sam doesn't seem the sort to do that. Of course, that's the whole problem. Sam isn't what he seems."

"I still don't understand."

"I thought he was unemployed, that his house was about to be condemned, and he needed money desperately."

"That's absurd. Where would you get an idea like that?"

"From you."

"Hey, wait a minute. I never said any of that."

"Not in so many words, but when you first suggested him before Thanksgiving to–" Trish's face turned toward the kitchen doorway, checking, Sam guessed, for little ears. "To do me that favor, you said he wasn't working, that he was staying with you because his house had holes in the floors and walls and wasn't safe, and that he might have to turn off his heat."

Jenny sat down hard, a stunned look on her face. Despite the circumstances, Sam fought a grin, wishing he had a camera. He'd never seen Jen speechless.

"Oh, I know the truth now." Trish waved a hand in dismissal. "The point is, Sam knew what I believed, and he used it against me."

Sam gritted his teeth. *I did not use you*, he wanted to shout. He wanted to go in and shake her. He wanted to say, "I'm sorry. I made a mistake. Now, forgive me, like you would Tyler or Jenny or anyone else you love, and get over it." But if he said that, she'd never speak to him again.

"For Pete's sakes, Trish. It's not like he's a serial killer or anything. He's a millionaire." Jenny chuckled. "This was a misunderstanding, right? What's the big deal?"

"Jenny, how can you not understand? He lied to me."

"Ah, now we're getting down to the real problem. You're blaming him for Duke's shortcomings."

"How can you even say that?"

"Well, it's true, isn't it? You're trying to protect yourself. You're dressing Sam in Duke's clothing, so to speak, because you're afraid Sam will be like him."

"That's ridiculous. I can't believe you'd say this to me."

"Somebody has to knock some sense into your head, friend, because you're confusing the issue."

"The issue," Trish said scathingly, "is that Sam told me what suited his purposes, and whether you understand it or not, I'm not going to tie myself to another manipulator."

Jenny folded her arms over her chest and raised her eyebrow at Trish.

"I'm not assigning him Duke's qualities," Trish said. "I'm not afraid to get married." Her voice broke, taking Sam's heart with it. "I was looking forward to a life with Sam."

They sat silent for so long Sam almost turned away. It was over. Trish couldn't forgive him.

"So, what happens now?" Jenny asked.

"Life goes on."

"At least you've got the store."

"Big deal."

Sam jerked in surprise. She took great pride in that store. Was he really that important to her? And if that was true, why had she given up on him?

Trish shrugged. "I'll need another you-know-who."

Jenny shook her head. "Bart will help you with Ty, but only Sam can fill *your* wish list."

*

Christmas Eve. Trish shook her head. She'd never dreaded a holiday this much in her life, not even right after Duke died. Tyler slept in his room down the hall, leaving her alone with more ghosts than had visited Scrooge.

Sam's spirit, her possible Christmas future, was a shape-shifter. He came as the beguiling handyman, needing her love to make him whole. Then the charismatic contractor appeared, hiding his money in his deep pockets. He lured her into foolishness, convincing her to trust again, only to watch him fade into the shadows like the shade he was.

Duke's grinning image haunted her with his faults and reminded her of his charming ways in Christmases past.

Jenny's imaginary spirit frightened her the most. She conjured a vision of Trish dancing with the wispy vapors of Duke's ghost for the rest of her life, spinning faster and faster, but afraid to break free.

Maybe it wasn't too late. Maybe, like Scrooge, she could change her present behavior and influence her future.

Trish considered Jenny's accusations again. Was she really punishing Sam for Duke's sins and hurting herself in the process?

Maybe it wasn't about Sam, after all. Maybe she needed to forgive Duke and let go of the past. Ready to try anything, she took a deep breath and said aloud, "Duke, I know you meant well. You did your best. Given the kind of person your mother is, you couldn't help using people. You didn't really know any other way. I understand now."

Her chest ached, filled to bursting with both love and regret that she'd never said this to him. "I forgive you, Duke. If I ever made you feel like you couldn't please me, I'm sorry."

Trish let the tears fall, feeling them ease her soul. She let go of the past, of all the hurt Duke had inflicted. She sat calmly for a few minutes as peace filled her heart and settled around her.

Now it felt like Christmas. Except she was alone. She looked at the clock. Almost eleven.

Her heart pinched. Bart, not Sam, would be here soon. She took a deep breath and vowed to call Sam tomorrow. She wanted him, yet she'd let her past with Duke color her experiences with Sam and make her unable to forgive him his mistake. Maybe, if she groveled, Sam would take pity on her for her short-sightedness. Surely he'd understand that she'd had some things to work out.

At 11:15, a quiet rap sounded at the front door. Checking out the window first, she opened the door to let in Santa.

"Hi, Bart." She peered closer. Dark blue eyes stared at her hesitantly through a cloud of white fuzz that could only belong to Sam, the one man she longed to see right now, and the one man she didn't expect. Her mouth went dry. Unable to express her delight, she stepped back and opened the door wider.

Sam walked in, never taking his gaze from hers.

"I'm glad you're in costume," she said.

"I didn't want Tyler to recognize me, and I thought it would be quicker."

Trish bit her lip, regretting that he want to get this visit over with. "I understand. Would you like a drink or something before you go see Tyler?"

"You think it'd be okay to take off the beard and hat?"

"Sure. Ty sleeps like a hibernating bear. What would you like?"

Sam pulled off his disguise. "Aren't I supposed to get milk and cookies?"

Relieved they could talk without bitterness, Trish smiled.

She brought in their snack. Sam sat on the couch, watching the lights on her Christmas tree blink. "Interesting tree."

Trish smiled and regarded the evergreen. Scrawny, drooping and almost needleless in places, it nonetheless brought cheer to the house. "Ty chose it. He takes Charlie Brown's example too much to heart. We'll probably always have a tree like this."

"You're lucky."

She glanced at Sam, who met her gaze for only a moment. Regret shadowed his eyes.

She set down her cup. "Sam, I'm so sorry."

"No, I'm sorry. I misled you."

She took his hand and squeezed it. "You didn't know about my past and my hang-ups." She swallowed. "Can we start over?"

He gathered her in his arms and hugged her tightly. Burying her face against his chest, she savored the strength of his body and the warm scent of his skin. She belonged in his arms and vowed never to leave.

"It's not your fault," he said against her hair. "I know what lying leads to." He eased her away. "I'll never lie to you again, even by omission. I promise. Give me another chance."

Trish placed her fingers over his lips. "You don't need to say anything." She smiled as he kissed her fingertips. "You've kept every promise you've ever made, including helping Ty with my present and coming here tonight, even thinking our relationship was over."

"But it's not over, right?"

"It's not. I don't want to be without you." Trish leaned into his embrace, kissing him with all the love in her heart. She tasted salt and realized she was crying happy tears. "Can you forgive me?"

"For what?" Sam asked against her mouth.

"For being so rigid and unforgiving." She forced herself to meet his gaze. "I love you so much I got scared. It's hard to be vulnerable again."

"I'll do my best not to hurt you. You won't regret loving me."

"Oh, Sam, I don't. I couldn't."

"Will you marry me?"

"Yes." She hugged him closer, unable to believe her Christmas wish had come true. Sam loved her. The three of them would be a family.

His mouth captured hers, branding her as his own.

After a few moments, she said, "I have something for you."

Sam chuckled. "You naughty, wonderful girl. But it'll have to wait. Duty calls."

"Not *that*. Well, yes, that, but something else, too."

He released her and straightened his red coat. "Trish, I already love Tyler as if he were my own son. When the time is right for all of us, including your in-laws, I'd like to adopt him."

Tears pricked her eyes. "He loves you, too."

"I hope so. I'm so lucky, getting you and Ty."

"We've been blessed, as well." She stood and reached toward him. "There's a little boy down the hall who needs Santa to visit him, but I've got something for you."

Trish picked up the box she'd wrapped, intending to take it to Jenny's. The quilt could only belong to Sam.

He took the box. "I wanted to give you an engagement ring for Christmas, but under the circumstances, I didn't think you'd accept."

She smiled. "Open it."

After pulling at the wide red satin ribbon, he lifted off the lid. He pushed back the tissue paper and stared at the quilt inside.

"Do you like it?"

"It's fantastic. You actually made this for me?"

Trish bit her lip. "I was worried you'd freeze if you couldn't pay your heating bill."

Sam met her gaze. His lips twitched as he fought a grin and lost.

Trish laughed with him, glad they could joke about it.

She stood and led the way to Tyler's room. She stopped outside his doorway, just out of view, to let Santa go in alone. But Sam wasn't behind her. She backed up a few steps toward the bathroom and smiled when she saw Sam tweaking his beard into place.

"Hey," Sam whispered to Trish's reflection in the mirror. "Don't mock me. This is important."

"You're the sweetest man I've ever known."

Taking a deep breath, Sam walked into Tyler's bedroom, conscious of Trish in the hall, peeking around the doorframe. Only Ty's night light illuminated the room, but Sam feared the room still might be bright enough to show him up for an imposter. He held Tyler's innocent beliefs, his hopes, dreams and trust in his hands.

Playing Santa was a good rehearsal for being a father.

As his eyes adjusted, Sam looked toward the bed. Tyler slept, not like a hibernating bear, but like a little angel. Long eyelashes rested against soft cheeks rounded with sleep and smoothed of the day's cares.

This child will be mine. Sam closed his eyes in a prayer of thanksgiving as love for the boy and his mother washed through him, both calming him and expanding his chest until it ached with joy.

He stepped forward and sat at the edge of the bed. He

reached out, intending to gently nudge Ty awake, but unable to resist stroking his fingers along Ty's cheek first. So warm and soft. Ty shifted and Sam moved his hand to the boy's shoulder. He cleared his throat, then gave Ty a little shake. He deepened his voice like a department store Santa. "Tyler."

The boy's lashes fluttered.

"Tyler Howell." Damn, he didn't know Ty's middle name. So much to learn, and thank God, now he'd have the chance to learn it all.

Ty rubbed his nose, then opened his eyes. They flew wider. "Santa?"

"Hello, Tyler."

"You're really here? You're really here!"

"Easy, now. Let's not wake your mother."

"Oh," Ty whispered, "right. I can't believe you came."

"Didn't you write me a letter, asking me to?"

Ty nodded.

"Well, here I am." Santa leaned closer. "And I brought your bike."

"Wow. Thanks, Santa."

"You're an especially good boy, Tyler. You do well in school and are always respectful to your mother."

Ty bit his lip. "I'm not always good."

"You mean dropping Horsey in the toilet? Ho, ho, ho." Sam held his belly as he laughed, trying to look jolly and keep his stomach padding in place. He grinned at Tyler's awed expression. "You didn't intend to do that."

His eyes widened. "You *do* know everything."

Sam gave in to the urge to ruffle Tyler's white-blond hair. "Tyler, I'm going to tell you something I don't get a chance to tell most boys and girls. Sometimes it's hard to believe in things. Like me, for instance. Your friends will tell you Santa doesn't exist."

"They did already. That's why I wrote you."

"Yes. I was able to come to you and prove myself, but I can't visit every child. I do have all those toys–and bikes–to deliver."

Ty grinned at the mention of bikes.

"There'll be other times when something's hard to believe in, times when you won't have anyone to write, times when something can't be proven to you."

Tyler frowned. "But how will I know it's real?"

"That's when you have to believe, just because you do. That's when you can't let other people tell you what's true. You'll have to feel the truth for yourself in your heart."

"I'll try, Santa, but it sounds hard."

"Of course it's hard. When you get back to school, the kids will still tell you I'm not real. You won't be able to prove that I came, will you?"

Tyler shook his head. "But I'll know."

"That's exactly what I'm telling you. Even when something seems impossible, you can still believe, because you know in your heart that it's true." Sam stood. "If you carry me in your heart, I'll always be real to you, no matter what anyone else says."

"I'll remember, Santa."

"Now, be a good boy and go back to sleep."

Tyler propped an elbow behind him. "Can't I get up, now that you've come?"

Sam shook his head a little, hoping the beard stayed on. "Your bike will still be in the living room in the morning, Tyler. Tonight I start keeping track of your behavior for next year's present."

Tyler fell back on the mattress, yanked the blanket to his chin and squinched his eyes shut. "Okay. G'night, Santa."

Sam stepped past Trish, who busily wiped tears from her eyes. He walked to the front door, opened it and then closed it again. He listened for sounds from the hall, but didn't hear Tyler get up or Trish move. A few minutes passed, and she didn't join him. He walked back to her as quietly as he could. "What's wrong?" he whispered.

Trish lifted his hand and placed it against her cheek. She feathered a kiss across his palm. "Nothing. You were perfect. I just want to make sure he goes back to sleep."

"He's really something, isn't he?"

Trish nodded, her face soft with sweet maternal pride. She laid her head against his chest. Sam wrapped his arms around her and stroked her hair, sharing the moment with her. This was what it meant to be a parent. Awe-filling love mixed with awesome responsibility for a fragile person, separate, and yet a part of you.

"I think he's sleeping," Trish whispered. She slipped quietly into Ty's room.

After waited for her nod, Sam walked in for another look. He stopped half-way across the room, letting Trish's body block him from Ty's view in case he awoke.

Sam backed a few steps away, granting her a private moment. Something drew his gaze to the window. He peered out to discover what had attracted his attention but only saw his reflection.

Must have been the snow falling. Large, puffy flakes floated from the sky, adding the perfect touch to Christmas Eve. Sam focused once again on his reflection. He looked better in the suit than he'd thought.

Then his reflection winked.

Sam froze, transfixed. The Santa in the window grinned, but Sam hadn't. Quickly, he glanced over at Trish. She was stroking Ty's hair, paying no attention to the mysterious appearance of Santa outside the window. Sam looked back, but saw only a fainter image of himself.

What had he seen? A trick of the light? Was it just his tired mind, stressed out by days of worry over losing Trish, conjuring up a fantasy?

Or could it have been...?

Excerpt from
Holly & Ivey: Christmas in Stilton, Book Two

December 21st

    Outrage fueled Holly McDonald as she sped to a showdown in the town she'd left at age twelve. Such a strong emotion made for an uncomfortable travel companion. Especially when headed to a wedding. Especially when she was the maid of honor. Especially four days before Christmas.

    Little white puffs flew out of the black of the night sky as wet snowflakes splattered the Toyota Corolla she'd borrowed. Holly turned up the defroster to remove fog from the windshield and cranked the heater to its hottest setting. Between her mission to stop her friend's wedding and the stiff, sideways Illinois wind buffeting the car and trying to push her into the other lane, she couldn't stop shivering. Fortunately, Stilton lay only a few miles ahead. After completing her task, shelter, hot food, and a warm bed topped her priority list. She couldn't think of her own comfort now, though. She had to get to Bree.

    A signboard along I-55 for the IVEY CHRISTMAS TREE FARM caught her eye. Her chill abated in the warmth of fond memories.

    Luke Ivey. She couldn't honestly say she'd thought of him in years. Once he'd been her closest pal, although they'd lost touch after she'd left Stilton. After his dad passed, he and his brother, Micah, had taken over running the Ivey Orchard, according to Bree.

Poor Bree. Her friend would be devastated when Holly told her what she'd seen a few days before in Chicago, after Bree had left for the holiday at home. From here on out, the Christmas season would always remind Bree of having her heart broken by Alan the Cheater.

***

Available in print and digital editions.

About the Author

Megan Kelly fell in love with romance books in her teens and sees no end in sight. Thank goodness! Getting paid to follow her passion is the best job ever.

She lives with her husband and two children in the Midwest, where the weather has an imagination–and sense of humor–of its own.

Please visit her website at megankellybooks.com.

A note from the author:

If you enjoyed this book, please post a review to the major online retailers and GoodReads or BookBub. Good reviews keep me in candy bars while I write.

To learn about my releases, sign up for my newsletter on my website. I don't send it out unless I have news to share. Subscribers receive a bonus short story in my "Love in Little Tree" series!

Thanks for reading,

Megan